SUSAN TERRIS

NELL'S QUILT

A Sunburst Book • Farrar, Straus and Giroux

For Amy

NELL'S QUILT

Sunday, February 26, 1899

No, no, never . . . No matter what they say. No matter what they do, I will *not* marry Anson Tanner.

That's what I told Papa and Mama when they informed me of Anson Tanner's proposal. Until that moment, the day had been a Sabbath like any other. We'd done morning chores and attended services at Unity Church in Amherst. Midday, foul weather had blown in from the northwest, keeping us indoors while wind and sleet battered the windows. As on many Sundays in the half year since my Grandmother Shaw's death, Mama had been trying to interest me or my younger sister, Eliza, in stitching on our grandmother's quilt fabrics.

Then Anson Tanner's name fell between us. Mama was tentative, but Papa sounded as if he were speaking about a brood mare in a transaction where he was getting the better half of a trade. I was outraged.

Mama, frowning at the vehemence of my reaction, turned away. She began to riffle through her mother's basket of silk and velvet scraps. My grandmother, who'd lived in Boston, had meant to make them into a crazy quilt, but she'd been so busy marching and campaigning for women's rights that she hadn't taken time to do it.

Glaring at the quilt fabrics, I once again informed my parents that I had no intention of marrying Anson Tanner. Not that he's a bad person. He isn't. He's a cousin twice removed of Papa's, a quiet and earnest soul who works in Hadley as manager of his family's shoe factory. Since his own papa's death, my father has been both friend and mentor to him.

I have nothing against Anson Tanner, except—oh, Nell, you petty person—I dislike the bluish shadows on his cheeks and chin when it's been too long since he's used his razor. In fact, I feel sorry for him, left a widower at twenty-four with a small child to raise. But not that sorry.

"Eleanor," Papa remonstrated, tamping on his pipe, "I'm surprised at this outburst. You've always been so steady. And for your age—mature—a grown woman. Besides, I know you're fond of Anson, and he cares for you."

"If *Eleanor* is a grown woman," Eliza said, "I must be old enough to put my hems down and my hair up." She was preening in front of the looking glass, fluttering one of my grandmother's Chinese paper fans before her eyes.

Since when, I asked myself, am I a grown woman? Is eighteen grown? I won't be finished with high school until June. And since when "Eleanor"? No one has ever called me anything except Nell. I turned toward Mama, but her eyes were still fastened on the basket full of patches. The house felt hot. I jumped to my feet and tugged at the collar on my dress. "I don't want to leave home. Or get married. Not now or ever."

"Then why do you talk about going to live in Boston?" Papa asked. "Is this the conversation of a person who doesn't want to leave home?"

"That's different," I said. "That's because I want to help people as Grandmother Shaw did."

Mama finally looked up. "Nell, the money that allowed your grandmother to do those things is gone."

I wanted to scream. There was too much talk about

of her. Rob even volunteered to carry her books so she wouldn't have trouble keeping up. This made me feel like chortling. If he ever offered to carry mine, I'd box his ears.

Eliza was pleased. I could tell by the way she flung her taffy-colored curls behind her shoulders and by the dots of pink that appeared on her cheeks as she deposited the books in his hands. With more decorum than if we'd been alone, we headed toward the brickyard, which was the source of the fire.

It was another cold, blustery day, part of an unseasonal freeze that started with the Sunday sleet storm and had lasted more than a week, but we were warm, because of the heat from the fire. Standing with school friends, we watched the firemen aim their hoses at the flames, then at adjoining structures to keep them watered down. First, word circulated through the crowd that the fire had been ignited by a kerosene lamp. The next rumor blamed a lit cigar.

Clusters of students from Amherst College and a few groups of Smith College women were there along with most of the town merchants, all of whom were thankful that it was someone else's business burning. When Marco the peanut man appeared, the gathering took on a party atmosphere. As Marco wheeled his charcoal-heated barrel amid the crowd, his skinny little monkey collected money and handed out packs of nuts.

Eliza stuck to us like a tick, but she kept complaining that it was too cold if we stood back from the fire and too hot if we stepped closer. Her feet were wet, she informed us, and she had to keep her left hand in her pocket because she only had one glove.

Rob and I exchanged glances. Rob fished down into his pocket and drew out a few loose coins. "Go ask Marco for some peanuts."

"But peanuts make me ill," Eliza said.

"Never mind. Do it," I told her. "They'll keep your hands warm!"

As soon as she turned and began to edge through the crowd, Rob and I scuttled off in the opposite direction. We cut through Magee's Blacksmith shop and fled down North Pleasant Street. As we ran, we waved at trolley passengers. Then, just beyond the train station, we crossed the tracks and headed across the winter-brown hills toward the pond, which we passed when we took the shortcut home.

Arriving breathless at its banks, we dropped the books on a frozen patch of ground and sat on a log. In season, this pond was a favorite place for ice skaters, but today it was deserted, and the ice looked less than trustworthy.

" 'Alone at last,' " Rob said, quoting a line from one of our favorite melodramas. "I've hardly seen you for days."

As soon as the words were out of his mouth, my high spirits began to seep away. My mouth felt dry and my stomach shivery as the name An-son Tan-ner beat a steady tattoo inside my head. I wanted to tell Rob, but I didn't know how to begin.

As I hesitated, he examined me. "You're looking peaky, Nell. Are you coming down with a fever?"

"Oh, no," I assured him. "I'm quite fine."

With a nod, he changed the subject. "Did you see them standing around at the fire?"

"Who?"

"The college students, of course."

This was a favorite topic of ours. Rob, who didn't think he wanted to go to college, though his family was prepared to send him, couldn't understand how I longed to be one of the Smith College women.

"I saw them," I said. "But it's useless to dream about something that's never going to happen."

"Aren't you going to ask your mother's people for help? Those sisters in Boston. We agreed upon that, didn't we?"

"Maybe."

"Not maybe—yes!"

"Perhaps . . ."

Rob shook his head. He wanted to go to sea or enlist as a soldier and fight in the Philippine revolt. He talked of leaving soon after our June graduation. Tobias would take up the slack, he said, so his folks wouldn't miss him any more than if he was at college.

"I'm thinking more about the sea and less about soldiering," he told me.

I grimaced. My Grandfather Shaw had been a sea captain. He'd died rounding Cape Horn on one of his return voyages from China. But Rob knew that. We'd been over this subject at least a thousand times.

"Oh, Nell, *I'd* never attempt the Straits of Magellan in a storm. Besides, I'll bring you trinkets when I return." Yes, he'd bring me trinkets. Our house was filled with Chinese objects brought by my grandfather. We had enough fans and teapots and perfume bottles to stock a store. And how had Grandmother Shaw felt waiting alone in Boston? Not lonely enough to spend her evenings by a fire stitching on a crazy quilt. Perhaps she had been too preoccupied with women's suffrage to care. But I care. Especially about what happens to Rob.

"Aren't you afraid of death, of dying?" I asked him, only half curious to hear his answer. What I was actually doing was procrastinating, as I tried to summon enough courage to mention Anson Tanner.

"Nell Edmonds! Since when are you so cautious? Since when do you—" All of a sudden, Rob turned and fixed his eyes on my face. "Wait, out with it. Something *is* wrong."

"Yes."

"What?"

"Anson Tanner wants to marry me," I said, trying to spit the words out quickly. "Mama and Papa believe I should."

"Now? Soon? I thought you were going to wait for me. Or that you'd shut yourself up like Miss Dickinson and write poems to an unknown lover."

"Your humor is inappropriate," I told him. "This is the most serious thing that's ever happened to me."

"No, it's not, Nell. Not really. Because you won't be marrying Mr. Tanner, and that's that."

"It isn't that simple, Rob. He's already spoken to Papa."

"Well, I'll go speak to your father. I'll tell him you can't."

"And he'll listen to you, I suppose?"

"Sure. Why not? I'll tell him you're not available—and that we're a pair."

"Not available? A pair? What kind of a pair? You're not going to be here, and I'll be alone." I covered my face with my hands. He didn't understand. "Besides, what are you talking about? You're my *friend*, Rob. Just my friend."

"I know, but . . ." His voice trailed off. He looked perplexed. He was only a seventeen-year-old boy. And what one could expect from a boy, I reminded myself, was limited. Because we were best friends, he believed I'd be spared from an unwanted marriage. How impossible. Clamping my lips together, I resolved to say no more on this subject.

Rob pulled off his blue cap and scratched his head. After a few moments, he began to rummage through the pockets of his jacket. Soon he produced a cold biscuit and an apple. "Here. Help yourself."

"No, thanks, I'm not hungry."

"Come on, it's good for you. An apple will put roses in your cheeks again." He pulled at the long braid that hung down my back. "Tobias won't like you if you're peaked, Nellie. Tobias says you're pretty, Nellie. Such a pretty girl."

Ever since Tobias had arrived, Rob had tormented me with lies about him. They'd never struck me as funny, and today they were particularly disagreeable. So, annoyed, I turned and toppled him off the log.

As soon as I'd done that, I was angry at myself. Rob wasn't responsible for my predicament or for his inability to understand it. I reached down to give him a hand.

By the time we were again seated side by side, I was hungry enough to take a bite from his apple. It was full of brown spots, and mealy from being stored too long in the root cellar. "Ugh," I said, spitting it out. Then I tossed it in the air, watching as it came down and skidded across the ice.

Rob jumped to his feet. "Just because you're not hungry doesn't mean I'm not."

I smiled. "If you want the apple, get it yourself."

He turned and looked down at me. "Is that a dare?"

We had, between us, a pact that every dare was to be taken seriously, so before I could say yea or nay, Rob was picking his way across the pond. The ice creaked and water oozed up at the shoreline, but he managed to retrieve the apple without breaking through.

As he approached me, I steeled myself for the fact that he was going to stuff it down my throat. But, to my surprise, he stopped and threw the apple out where it had been before. "Now it's your turn, Nell. Go after it. *I* dare *you!*"

It was sheer foolishness. I knew that right from the beginning, yet I didn't hesitate. Recklessly, I began to make my way across the unstable ice. Rob and I are the same height, but he's slight and wiry. I must outweigh him by ten pounds or more.

The frozen surface bubbled under my boots as it had done under his; yet, if I was careful, I was sure I'd be able to get hold of it. As I bent for the apple, I could tell that the ice ahead was thinner. Balancing precariously, I reached out.

One boot slid sideways. There was an instant when I caught myself, thought I'd be all right. I was mistaken. With a creaking sound, the pond opened up to receive me.

Since the pond is shallow, I was not in danger, but I was stuck in frigid mud, and Rob had to come help. Almost immediately, he went through the ice, too. What a silly predicament. Holding on to one another, we shrieked with laughter as we dragged ourselves out of the muck and staggered off over the fields toward our homes.

We should have been distraught. But, except for the fact that we were chilled to the bone, we were fine.

"What a day," Rob kept repeating. "First fire and then ice. Fire and ice, fire and ice."

Every time he spoke, I laughed again.

I was still chuckling when I stepped in at the kitchen door and dropped my books and Eliza's onto the counter. Mama took one look at me and she turned into a harridan. "You're disgraceful! Do you think you're still twelve years old? Liza's been home for ages, but you—look at you, Nell! You're getting everything filthy."

Eliza, I could see, was lurking in the side hall, delighted that I was getting the comeuppance I deserved for deserting her.

"You've ruined my floor," Mama said.

"I'll mop it," I promised her. "As soon as I change. It was an accident. I'm sorry."

"You're too old for this, you know. Too old to be cavorting through the countryside with Rob Hoffman."

"I'm sorry," I repeated.

"And you were supposed to churn the butter for me."

"Oh, the butter," I replied giddily. I was, by now, shivering so hard I couldn't make my tongue obey. "The butter. How could I have forgotten the b-b-butter? But why do we have to make butter? W-w-why don't we buy it in town as other people do?"

"Because," Mama said, "we need the butter money as much as we need the egg money and the money from the sugaring."

Oh, money again. Always money. I tried to keep my face under control. I almost managed to do so, too, except my mother said something that set me off once more.

"What," she asked, "would Anson Tanner say if he could see you now?"

I opened my eyes very wide. "Why, M-m-mama," I replied, "I suppose he'd say I'm too young to marry!"

Then, cackling insanely, I slipped past her and ran off toward my room.

⊞

Sunday, March 19, 1899

Today Anson Tanner, his mother, and his red-haired daughter, Jewel, shared our midday dinner with us. Mrs. Tanner seemed to be evaluating me as a prospective daughter-in-law, but she spoke little except to declare she did not believe in cosseting the young. Later, when the meal was finished, we sat together, awkwardly attempting to while away the rest of the afternoon.

When I say "we," I speak of everyone except Mama, who remained in the kitchen scouring the pots and pans. Although I offered to help, she refused. It was my duty, she whispered between clenched teeth, to preside in the parlor as hostess.

My duty, as far as I was concerned, extended no further than to see each person had a cup of tea. Once that was accomplished, I was determined to let family and guests fend for themselves.

At last, to my relief, Papa and Anson Tanner fell into their accustomed intimacy and began to exchange views on the upcoming Presidential election and the state of the nation's economy. Another time, I'd have joined in their discussion, but today I did not wish to participate in anything which might give the impression I wanted to please Anson Tanner.

He had not yet broached the subject of marriage to me, hesitating, perhaps, because of his shyness. Never—since I reached the age of fourteen—has he allowed his gaze to meet mine. His conduct and demeanor are always beyond reproach. Today, the most off-putting thing about him was that he crossed his legs so I could see curls of dark hair between his stocking top and his trousers. But that's being uncharitable. When I am generous, I'm forced to admit that he's nearly as handsome as my sister believes he is.

Jewel, on the other hand, except for the astonishing red hair, has none of the beauty that her name might imply. She's a wizened thing of four, with arms and legs as thin as saplings. I chose to ignore her, so Eliza, who professes to be smitten with children, took the child under her wing. As I sipped my tea, they examined the perfume bottles, bits of porcelain, and chinoiserie from Grandfather Shaw.

The tea was refreshing, especially as I'd eaten little at dinner. My usually hearty appetite has declined over the last few weeks. Tonight the ham seemed too fatty and the yams underdone. After my second cup of tea, when I realized that I could not hide behind a biography of suffragist Lucy Stone for the entire evening, I scanned the parlor until my eyes lit upon the basket of crazy-quilt fabrics.

I reached out and took it into my lap. I didn't intend to sew, just to make the time pass. Sewing, like many other farm chores, is simply something which has to be done. There's endless white work, socks to be darned and shirts to be mended. Bed quilts serve a purpose, but we have enough of those to last two lifetimes. A crazy quilt is different, a project for an old woman or an idle one, since the finished work is ornamental and has no use at all.

In the basket, along with the fabrics, I found packets of brightly colored embroidery threads and tissue transfers with designs for decorating quilt patches. I pushed these items aside and fixed my attention on the textiles. Where had Grandmother gone in the robin's-egg velvet? To what meeting with Lucy Stone or Anna Howard Shaw had she worn the wine-striped taffeta? Had she carried a matching parasol with it? Or, perhaps, a protest sign?

My reverie was interrupted when Mama appeared in the parlor. Before I knew what was happening, I was being asked to take Jewel for a walk. I wanted to refuse, but I couldn't. Mama looked tired and irritable, as if she were about to get her monthlies. I had mine, and she and I frequently shared similar dates.

Once I was out, though, I was relieved. Jewel was a decent walking companion, quiet and undemanding. The hills were greening up, and it was a glorious day. The early-spring sun spilled down, providing so much warmth that I needed only a shawl for my shoulders. Soon I unbuttoned Jewel's coat and let it hang loose.

We strolled past the barn, the coop, the washhouse, and other sheds. We'd had a cold night followed by a warm day, so the sap buckets had been hung in the sugar bush. I hoped I might find Rob there, but the sole person we spied was Tobias's wife waddling out the end of her pregnancy. I greeted her pleasantly, yet she behaved as if she had neither seen nor heard me.

"What's wrong with her?" Jewel asked.

"She's unwell," I answered.

Jewel wasn't satisfied. "No, there's something else. She's fat. Granny Tanner's fat, and you're fat, but *her* fat is all in one place."

"Well, compared to a rag doll like you," I told her, "the whole world looks fat."

Before the child could ask more questions about Tobias's wife, I dipped my hand into a sap bucket. "Here. Taste. It's maple sugar."

Jewel looked skeptical. "Maple sugar comes from the Grange Store. Granny Tanner and I buy it there."

"Go on, taste." By now the sap had begun to seep through my fingers, dripping onto the ground.

At last, Jewel, like a little bird, dipped her mouth down and sipped. "It tastes maple-y," she admitted.

"Try it again."

"But I don't believe that's what it is."

"Well, don't," I said irritably. My fingers were sticky, and I was forced to lick them clean myself. I'd always loved the taste of uncooked sap, but today I found its thin sweetness cloying.

Jewel waited until I had wiped my hand upon my skirts. Then, with maddening fickleness, she asked for a second taste. It was all I could do to avoid thrashing her. Urging patience upon myself, I lifted her up and allowed her to reach into a bucket. A moment later, I plunked her down and began to stride from the woods toward the orchard. Jewel trailed silently behind me.

Even though I was wearing my Sunday slippers, I kicked at stones in my path. After a while, yielding to another impulse, I swung from the low-hanging limb of an apple tree. The tight buds on the branches above gave promise of green leaf and blossoms. I could cut some, take them inside, and force them to bloom. But I wouldn't. I preferred them swaying in the orchard.

Feeling more like myself, I turned back to Jewel. Her face was glazed with maple sap and caked with dirt she'd acquired from some occupation I hadn't observed. She looked so waiflike that I took pity on her.

"We have a swing over there. Would you like to swing?"

She shook her head. "No."

"Come on. I'll push you."

"No."

"Why not?" I asked.

"Granny Tanner doesn't let me."

"Why not?"

"Because I might get dirty. Or hurt."

I shook my head in disbelief. "What do you do with your granny when your papa is at work?"

"Nothing," she answered, rubbing one grubby fist against her cheek.

"Doesn't she play with you?"

"No, she's old as white thread, and her heart pains her. If I speak too much, her head does, too."

Poor Jewel. Anson Tanner was right to think she needed someone to mother her. What a shame he thought it should be me.

The child tugged at the collar of her frock. "Does your head hurt when I talk?"

"No," I said.

Then, like a newly opened bottle of ginger beer, she began letting words bubble from her lips. "Pappy said you have horses here. Do you? Can I see them? And a cow you get milk from? Is this truly an apple orchard? And if it is, why are there no apples? Our apples don't come from orchards, you know. Or our milk from a cow."

Impulsively, I grabbed the child and loped toward the swing. Soon we were swinging together, with the branches of the apple tree creaking about our heads. Jewel was facing me, her legs curved one on either side of my hips. While we glided back and forth, her curly red head rested on my breast.

That's how we were when Anson Tanner found us. I was tempted to leap from the swing, thrust his daughter into his arms, and disappear downhill into the woods. Instead, I stayed put.

Mama would be aghast if she saw me swinging like a child while my would-be bridegroom stood before me. Anson Tanner didn't seem to mind, however. He shuffled his feet. He leaned against one of the trees and gazed out over the woods and fields.

As he stood there, a sharp breeze blowing in from the west made his eyes tear up. Instead of brushing the tears away, he remained as he was.

"Look at me, Pappy," Jewel called when she caught sight of him.

"I see," he replied, drawing his handkerchief from his pocket.

At that moment, a curious notion occurred to me. Perhaps Anson Tanner didn't need a wife. Perhaps what he wanted was a housekeeper, someone young and strong to breathe life into his poppet of a daughter. I was a good housekeeper. Quite a competent one, as a matter of fact. Soon Jewel could start at grammar school, and while she was at school I could be at college, using the housekeeper's wages to pay my fees.

With Jewel's hard head bouncing on my chest, the idea made perfect sense. My only misgiving came when I chanced to see Rob over by the Hoffmans' barn. Hands on his hips, he was staring at us in disbelief. If he'd been close by, he would have told me that I should not marry Anson Tanner or become his housekeeper. He would have reminded me how little I cared about children.

I shut my eyes, so I would not have to see him or take heed of his words. I could be a *very* good housekeeper, and that would be my solution to the problems vexing me. What I needed, as soon as possible, was a chance to discuss this with Mama.

My eyes were still closed when Anson Tanner began to speak. "You are an admirable person, Nell," he said. "Strong. Healthy. And your father tells me you know what I wish to ask of you."

Tuesday, March 21, 1899

Anson Tanner's face-to-face offer of marriage had been as untimely as the March snows that have continued to plague us, and this afternoon, as Rob and I tramped home over last night's dusting of snow, I knew I planned to reject it. I meant to counter his proposal with mine.

My head was teeming with arguments to support the notion that I could become his housekeeper instead of his wife, when Rob suggested that we stop to skip stones on the thawed pond.

"Well . . ."

"Just for a minute," he urged.

I knew I shouldn't dawdle, because Mama, busy with the sugaring, needed my help, but I did. I wanted to consult Rob, see if he thought I could convince everyone that I was suited to be the Tanners' housekeeper.

"You're standing firm?" he asked, speaking up before I did. "You aren't going to marry Mr. Tanner?"

I turned sideways and launched a smooth, flat stone. "No, I think not, but . . ." When I tried to speak, I found that the words clotted in my throat.

"But what?"

"Nothing. Forget it."

Rob would make fun of the idea and mock me. It was better, I decided, to speak with my mother. He needn't know until the details had been arranged. So, instead of explaining what was weighing on my mind, I pointed out two red-winged blackbirds at the marshy end of the pond and a yellow crocus pushing its head up through the snow.

A short while later, swathed in a work apron, I stood at the edge of the outdoor fireplace helping Mama and Eliza remove gray scum from the tops of the boiling pots of maple sap. This was Eliza's favorite of the seasonal household tasks. As long as I took charge of keeping lengths of cordwood in the fire and assumed the responsibility for stoking it, Eliza was happy to keep stirring for hours on end.

In front, where the fire was hottest, we kept the fresh pots of sap, and in the rear the already condensed syrup continued to reduce even more. Ordinarily, I was delighted when my sister pitched in and carried her share of the work, but today it was irritating because I wished to speak with Mama alone.

Just as I was giving up hope that this could ever happen, Mama came to my aid. "Why don't you duck inside," she asked my sister, "and fix something to tide us over? When we finish here, we have ironing to do."

Eliza, her face pinkly moist from the heat and unaccustomed exertion, agreed. Mama said Eliza should add coal to the kitchen stove and put on the supper stew while she was there. "Don't come back," Mama cautioned, "until you're sure that the heat is evened out and won't scorch the pot."

The moment Eliza disappeared into the kitchen, Mama put down her wooden spoon and tugged at the bodice of my dress. "Look at you, Nell. What's happening to you? A month ago this dress fit snugly. Now look how loose it is."

"It's always been loose," I insisted. "It's the rose-colored one that fits tightly."

I twisted out of her grasp. This was supposed to be *my* conversation, not Mama's. "I'm fine."

"No, you're not. And if things don't improve I'm going to ask Dr. Sternhagen to prescribe some tonic for you."

"I don't need tonic."

"Well, you need something. You're moping—not eating well, not sleeping. Your bed creaks at night as you toss and turn. I wish you'd stop procrastinating and give serious consideration to Anson's offer."

I wanted to tell her what I'd worked out, but her words made me angry, and, for the moment, my intentions flew from my head. "Is this an order? Do I *have* to marry him?"

Mama's answer was immediate. "No, Nell, it's up to you. This is your decision. But he's a good man—who can offer you a good life. He's gentle, temperate. You care for him. And . . ."

"And what?"

". . . he'll be able to provide for you well."

"So that's it—the good provider? Well, I suppose I should be grateful for a good provider."

"Did I say that, Nell?"

"That was your gist."

"Let's not argue, Nell, please. There's work to be done. Always work. Listen. I don't want you to live my life. I'm not yet forty, and look at me. For you—for you, for Eliza—I want something better."

Examining Mama, I didn't have the heart to keep arguing with her. She was pretty enough, but faded and round-shouldered. She looked like a blossom that had been cut, then left out of water too long.

"Mama," I said, gesturing with the long spoon, "I *have* made up my mind about Anson Tanner." I smiled, to re-assure her that I was about to offer good news.

"You have? Well, tell me, then."

Before I could begin, we were interrupted, as Tobias, accompanied by the Hoffmans' spaniel, lumbered up. From his shoulders a yoke was suspended, and on it hung two sap buckets. Mama steadied the yoke. Then she reached out for one of the buckets. Our sap came from the Hoff-mans' woods. They gave us what they couldn't use.

Tobias lowered his eyes and sniffed as I took hold of the second heavy bucket. The moment its weight was in my hands, he lurched, tipping the yoke against my breasts. Startled, I staggered backward, alarmed to find his eyes examining my body.

Mama, anxious to hear my words, had noticed nothing. "Thank you, Tobias," she said. "You're very helpful."

The moment he was out of earshot, she urged me to speak. Trying to collect my wits and forget about Tobias, I stalled for a moment or two. Then, as Mama was shifting a kettle to a cooler spot on the fire, I told her how I wished to be Anson Tanner's housekeeper and use my wages to go to college.

Mama stumbled. The fire hissed as thickened syrup slopped over the edges of the off-balance kettle. When I reached out to right it, its edge seared my hand.

I gasped.

"Are you all right?"

"Yes," I said. Although my hand seemed to be on fire, I denied feeling any pain.

If I had expected Mama to be pleased by my idea, I was mistaken. Instead, her pale eyes bulged. "Are you daft, Nellie?"

"Of course not."

"But, honeypot, there's something here you don't understand."

"Like what?" I asked. Moving a few steps away, I submerged my hand in a bucket of water that stood beneath the yard pump.

"Anson wants a *wife*."

"No," I told her. "I think you're wrong. He wants someone to cook and sew and take charge of Jewel."

Mama pulled some pins out of her hair. She twisted a stray wisp around the bun at the nape of her neck. As soon as she let go, however, the same lock fell down in front of her eyes again.

"Anson," she said, speaking slowly, "is not some frail old widower. He's only twenty-eight."

"I know."

Mama turned her face away and began to pour fresh sap into one of the front cauldrons. "Oh, Nell, Anson doesn't want a housekeeper. He and his mother already have one. He wants . . . a man wants. . . . You see, Anson has a man's requirements, and he wants someone who will be his wife. Someone who will perform the duties of a wife."

Alarmed, I pulled my hand from the bucket and used it to dribble cold water over my face. "The duties of a wife?" The words were no sooner out of my mouth than I knew I'd spoken too soon.

I couldn't mind Jewel and go to college. The whole notion had been a childish soap bubble. If I chose not to marry Anson Tanner, I didn't have any other options. I couldn't run away to join the army or go to sea. My stomach churned disagreeably. And my scalded hand hurt, too. As I was patting it against my apron, Eliza rejoined us, bringing raisins and slices of cinnamon bread.

"I wouldn't come out," she said, "till I was sure Tobias had gone. I don't like the way he looks at me."

Neither Mama nor I offered any response.

Eliza didn't seem to notice that she had blundered into the middle of a personal discussion. Dimpling, she put a hand on my shoulder. "Let's dip the bread in the hot syrup, Nellie. Oh, Nell, Nell—why didn't we get Jewel on our way home from school? We should have brought her out to see us cook the syrup. We could have gathered snow, too, and let the syrup harden in it as we used to do!"

At the mention of Jewel's name, my stomach contracted

again. Jewel, after all, had been borne by Lillian, who *had* performed the duties of a wife. As the sow to the shoat, as the hen to the rooster, as the mare to the stallion, as the tabby to the tom.

Eliza bent forward and lowered a slice of bread into one of the cooler pots at the rear. Mama chose that moment to lean forward and catch me by the hand. Her fingers were strong. I could feel the calluses on the palm of her hand. "We'll talk later," she promised. "I can help you understand. About requirements and—"

Before she could finish, I began to retch. Waves of nausea rolled through my body. Extricating myself from her grip, I ran back toward the privy. My unburned hand was out, reaching for the door, when I saw him.

Tobias. Tobias was there. What was he doing loitering near our privy?

"No," I moaned. "I can't. No . . ."

Trembling, I dropped my head and vomited on my feet.

Monday, April 24, 1899

Another Monday—another washday. Instead of spending Mondays in the barn or in the fields, Papa usually helps Mama by hauling water and emptying tubs as she does the laundry. I've always admired him for being willing to assist in women's work, but today, when I came upon him in the yard, I found myself wondering why he never helps Mama with any other chores.

I was in a dismal mood. Rob had not waited for me

after school, and Eliza—claiming to feel poorly after the exhausting ordeal of spring cleaning—had never left her bed. Was she ailing, I asked myself. Or did she simply wish to escape from the onerous tasks of washday?

In any case, because of Eliza, I'd have twice my usual Monday's work. Everything was off-schedule anyway, because Mama had spent half the morning dyeing the parlor curtains, turning them from pewter to pea-green. Now I'd be dragging the tubs of wash and unpinning already dried garments from the line until after sunset. As I passed my parents on the way to change into my work clothes, I greeted them tersely.

Nor was I pleased to encounter my sister. She had managed to drag herself downstairs to the parlor, where she was sitting on the floor with my grandmother's quilt fabrics. She was assembling them, holding them next to her bosom as if they were frocks she intended to wear to some Beacon Hill ball. When she caught sight of me, she sighed and pressed one hand to her forehead.

"Are you any better?" I asked. But before she could frame an answer, I walked away.

While I was up changing, I glanced out the open window to where Mama was stirring the last washload over a small wood fire. These garments had been soaked and scrubbed once. After the boiling they would require one last wash, a rinse, and the bluing. As Mama labored, Papa leaned against the pump, puffing at his pipe and waiting to be asked to fetch or drain water.

They were talking, and their words drifted up to where I stood.

"If I had even one extra penny," Mama said, "I'd use it to hire someone."

"But we don't. At least not now."

"I know."

"I'm sorry, Faith. Truly, when I took you from Boston, I didn't mean for your days to be this way."

"I know. I know."

"Perhaps," Papa said, "if Nell . . . though it's *her* choice . . . decides . . ."

"Hush!" Mama told him. "We mustn't."

I didn't wait to hear anymore. Turning away, I bolted from my room and pounded down the stairs. In the hall, momentarily dizzy, I stopped and steadied myself against the chest that stood under the looking glass.

When the prickling black dots subsided, I was startled to see my sister's face staring back at me. But, no, it was my face, looking angular like Liza's, rather than rounded like mine. I blinked and moved closer.

The old adage "Pretty is as pretty does" had always seemed sensible to me, but perhaps my face had been changing for years, and I'd never even noticed. I'd meant to hurry outside, yet I stayed before the glass, unwilling to move. After a few minutes, I tightened the sash on my dress. On impulse, I pulled the ribbon from the end of my braid and spread my hair about my shoulders. One of grandmother's fans was on top of the chest. I picked it up and flicked it past my eyes.

Oh, no, that was all wrong. I could not be coy and saucy like Eliza. My hair was straight, not softly wavy like my sister's. It was darker, too. And my face—I'd been mistaken—was round as ever with its unattractive chipmunk cheeks. I let the fan drop from my fingers.

It was then that I noticed Eliza standing in the parlor doorway, an afghan about her shoulders. Her Cheshire-cat grin made my stomach tighten, and once awakened, it began to growl, reminding me of how little I'd eaten that day. But, instead of giving in to hunger, instead of allowing my sister to see *me* shirking washday tasks, I forced myself to walk through the kitchen and out to the yard.

When I volunteered to run the last washload across the scrubboard, Mama refused. She said the soap chemicals were too harsh, and that she didn't want them to ruin my hands as they had ruined hers.

"Besides," she added, "you help enough around here. Washing is my duty. It's my responsibility."

Her words made me wince, so I turned away. Mama's tone when she talks about responsibility is not bitter—only resigned. As far as I can tell, she loves Papa, even if she doesn't always love the work that faces her each day. Resignation, however, is not for me. I want something different, something—

"Nell? Nellie?"

Papa was standing beside me. "Why don't we do the wringing together?" he suggested.

"Yes, fine," I agreed.

As we began to twist the water out of his heavy work clothes, I sank back into my own thoughts. When I tried to imagine myself wringing out clothes with Anson Tanner, I couldn't get the picture to focus, because if I were married to him, I wouldn't have to do the laundry. Mama wouldn't either, I realized suddenly. So that's what Papa meant before. If he and Mama weren't paying for *my* food, *my* upkeep, they'd have enough money to hire the washerwoman Mama wanted so badly.

And her life would be better. Well, that was one reason to marry. Could I give up my dreams of college and of

Boston for Mama? No. Well, perhaps, if I could find other equally convincing reasons to marry. But were there any others? I didn't love Anson Tanner. Or did I? I was fond of him.

Was that love? It was certainly different from the comradeship I felt for Rob. If I chose to marry, would my responsibilities as a wife be as terrible as some of the duties I performed as a daughter? While I was mentally cataloguing these daughterly duties, I was pressed into one of my least favorite ones when Mama cried out that the rooster had escaped again.

"Devil! Demon!" I called, chasing after him. He squawked, and the hens in the coop, alarmed by the fracas they could see but not hear, cackled stupidly.

Mama and Papa were smiling, but I wasn't. I loathe that mean, intemperate creature. Given half a chance, he'd peck a person's eyes out, and no pen devised by man can keep him in if he wants to get free.

"Go back in there," I cried, "before I wring your ugly neck!"

Finally, with Papa's help, I managed to corner him, chase him back where he belonged. Papa took charge then, fetching pliers, rebending the wire the rooster had loosened to make his escape. Catching him was one more of the never-ending, time-consuming responsibilities of farm life.

No matter how I attempted to evade them, they pressed in on me. And responsibility was what day-to-day living was about. Pipe dreams of college and of living in Boston were just that—puffs of smoke which would vanish in the slightest draft. Without money, certain things were impossible. That the rooster would find a new way to escape was a fact. That I could go to college or Boston was a dream. As unreal as my notion of being Anson Tanner's housekeeper.

Maybe, I decided, I would have to abandon impractical dreaming and fashion for myself a future that was, if not perfect, at least acceptable. Anson Tanner was not crude like Tobias. He would be kind.

Without me in the house, there might be money enough not only for a laundress but for a hired woman, someone to do the hard work I tried to take off Mama's shoulders. My work and more, if she was there all day, instead of in school as I was.

Still thinking, I lifted the basket of wrung-out clothes and carted it to the place between the house and the garden where the lines were hung. Dropping the basket, I stood for a moment watching already dried garments flap in the late-afternoon breeze. Nightgowns, shirts, petticoats, shifts. It was hypnotic. I stood there mesmerized. When I lowered my lids, I discovered that the lines sprang to life.

Right before my eyes, they became ghostly men and women, dancing as if their lives depended upon it. I couldn't tell if it was a dance of joy or of desperation, but I was impelled to be part of it. I began to run up and down between the lines of white spirits. Amid them, I was invisible. I couldn't see Mama, Papa, or anyone.

I was light as air, light-headed, too, as if the burdens around my heart had slipped away and would never return. A white work shirt embraced me as I passed. I spun around and honored it with a bow.

Then, absorbed by what seemed to be a portion of an intricate quadrille, I turned in the opposite direction. Suddenly, a striped nightshirt enfolded me in its flapping arms. It pressed its pliable, sun-warmed length against mine. For a moment, alarmed, I drew back. But, reconsidering, I responded by stepping closer, sighing.

"Yes," I cried out. "Yes, yes—I will."

"Stop it! Stop!" Papa insisted. Appearing from nowhere, he took hold of my shoulders and parted me from my pale partner. "What's come over you?"

"Let go of me," I demanded. I could smell tobacco on his breath. His fingers seemed to be burning a brand onto my upper arms. I pulled away. "Don't touch me. Let go. I want—"

"What *has* come over you?"

"I want . . ." The words were in my head. I'd heard them as the nightshirt held me. I needed to bring them to my lips and tongue. I would be better off. Mama would, too. With a hired woman to help, Mama would have a new life, an idyllic one.

Retreating from Papa, I turned back toward the garments straining on the clotheslines. Before me was my own nightdress. When I reached up, it billowed in the wind, and collapsed obediently in my arms. "There now, there," I crooned as I unpinned it.

Some dreams were the wrong dreams. But Nell—Nell the Good, Nell the Strong—could find the right dreams and cleave to them. Steady Nell understood the dreams that would make everyone happy.

I smoothed the nightdress against my chest. "I want— Mama, Papa. I want . . . no, that's not it, either. Not 'I want,' but I *will* marry Anson Tanner!"

Even as the declaration escaped from my mouth, I knew I wished to suck it back in, trap it between my teeth, and to eat so sparingly and have become so light I can borrow her dresses if I wish. That way, when I am gone from this house, Mama won't be without help. So I'm trying to strengthen Eliza, wean her from feigning illness, from spending too much time reading romances borrowed from her schoolmates. Today, to further this scheme, I rose early, left the house, and went into the woods to look for mush-rooms.

It was cool, but there was no wind. Pale spring leaves arched above my head. My hair, escaping from its loose nighttime braid, fell in tangles about my shoulders. I breathed shallowly, trying not to crush blades of grass and wildflowers beneath my feet. I found few mushrooms, but I knew what I was doing, because by the time I returned home, the nearly empty pail swinging in my hand, the morning chores would be done. They would be finished because Eliza will have had to do them.

Wandering with no fixed purpose except to ward off the morning chill, I came upon a shaded dell of violets. They were blooming in haphazard profusion almost as far as my eye could see. Awed by their beauty, I sank down and began to pick them, intending to take a nosegay home to brighten up Mama's day. I'd hardly begun when Rob announced his presence by calling my name as he came forging through the underbrush. I was provoked to find him there.

"What?" I asked.

"What are you doing?"

"What does it look like?"

"You're picking flowers. Are they for me? To say how much you've missed my company? Or are they for Mr.

Tanner? Since you're wearing his ring, I suppose they should be for him."

"Go away," I said, piqued by his words and by his tone of voice.

"Come on, Nell, stop it. You can't keep avoiding me forever."

I had been avoiding him—ever since my betrothal to Anson Tanner had been announced. Rob was appalled by my decision, and I couldn't bear to have him badger me.

This morning I'd been careless. He must have been watching when I left the house and followed me.

"It's no use," I told him. "We have nothing to talk about."

Instead of arguing, he knelt down and started to collect his own bunch of violets. For several minutes, neither of us said a word. Then—in a voice both tight and angry—he broke the silence. "This is all wrong, Nellie. Tell him. Tell them. You've made a *terrible* mistake."

I didn't look up. Struggling to contain myself, I continued to snap more violets from amid their heart-shaped leaves.

"Nell?"

When I answered, I spoke firmly. "It's not a mistake, Rob. I'm doing the right thing. I've made my decision, and I shall live with it."

"But it wasn't supposed to happen this way."

"Let's talk about something else," I suggested.

"Let's not."

"All right. Have it your way. How *was* it supposed to happen?"

Rob edged closer to me. "I'm not sure," he admitted. "But I've been thinking. And I've decided you should wait for me."

Friday, June 23, 1899

Last week was my high school graduation. Now I don't have to be with Rob every day. Now I only have three things to do—help at home, work on my quilt, and prepare for my marriage to Anson Tanner. Because we've been so busy, the quilt and wedding plans are proceeding at a snail's pace. It's always hectic on a farm, but summer is the worst season. Even with Papa hiring dayworkers in the fields, we never seem to get caught up.

This morning Mama, Eliza, and I—wearing bonnets to protect our faces—were stooped over in the garden. Jewel was with us. The garden was as good a place as any to be. As long as I'm not alone, I know Rob will keep his distance. Doing work in the hot sun is preferable to being with him and listening to his unwelcome opinions.

"It's a scorcher," Mama said, with an apologetic gesture, "but we must do the weeding before the garden chokes to death."

Eliza sighed. "I can't stay here any longer. My head is aching and I feel ill. But I'll take Jewel inside. I'll amuse her. Then, maybe later—"

"Later it will be even hotter," Mama said.

For a moment, I was tempted to accuse Eliza of being a malingerer, but I didn't. As I was learning patience and self-control, she, too, would have to learn. "Rome wasn't built in a day," I said.

"What?" my sister asked.

"Never mind," I said.

Mama nodded at Eliza. "Go ahead and rest. You needn't worry about Jewel. We'll keep her with us."

I wanted to protest, but I curbed my unworthy inclinations. This was extremely satisfying and so different from my usual hasty, willful methods that I felt as if I were accomplishing something monumental.

Biting my lip, I watched as Eliza trudged off toward the house. Then I allowed myself to think about Rob again. He and I have never settled our differences. In fact, the crevasse between us is growing wider. But that suits my purposes. It's easier than explaining over and over that I intend to marry Anson Tanner and become Jewel's mother.

It was Jewel herself who brought me back to the present. "What's growing out there?" she asked.

"Onions," I told her. "We sell them. My papa tends the onion fields. But here, in the kitchen garden, we grow beets, carrots, potatoes . . ."

"Is that all?"

"No, also pumpkins, turnips, and squash. And tomatoes."

"Is *that* all?"

I was getting more accustomed to the child and to her endless questions.

"Yes."

"I don't believe you," she said, pulling on the edge of her calico poke bonnet. "I don't see any pumpkins. I don't see any carrots."

"The pumpkins aren't formed yet," I explained, "and the carrots grow underground. These feathery leaves here are the carrot tops."

Then, turning away, I resumed weeding. Mama's dotted muslin was drenched with perspiration. I wished there was some way to spare her this work as we had spared Eliza.

"Mama . . ." I said.

"Yes, Nellie?"

"We should make Eliza help."

"I know," she agreed, using one forearm to wipe her forehead. "But there will be time enough after you're married."

I was surprised to see that Mama understood the problem, too. Perhaps I might have an ally as I attempted to make Eliza into some version of myself.

For a while, we worked in silence. The only sound was a low rumbling in my stomach. It was protesting because I'd skimped on breakfast again, but I refused to give in to hunger or to the fact that my fingers were sore from plucking at the stubborn, sharp-edged garden invaders.

At last, Mama spoke. "Nell. Tell me something."

"Of course, if I can."

"You're looking changed, slenderer yet womanly. Watching you with Jewel here and with your quilt in the evenings, I feel you've grown more serene. Is that true? Am I right?"

Her questions disturbed me. I wasn't sure how to answer them. But I was saved. Before I could reply, Jewel demanded my attention.

"See what I found," she called.

What I saw when I turned my head was alarming yet droll. Jewel had pulled our carrots one by one and laid them out in the sun.

"But they're very wee," the child said. "If we soak them in water, will they grow?"

By the time the carrots had been tamped back into the earth and we'd had dinner, Jewel was exhausted. I wanted to put her up in my room to nap, but Eliza—who'd been upstairs all morning—insisted that it was too hot.

"Even too hot to read. We can't stay in the house. We should go to the pond. The marshy end. If there's a breath of air off the water, it'll cool us down."

It wasn't a bad idea, except that it meant I had to be with Eliza, and I was peeved with her.

"Yes—go," Mama said. "We'll finish weeding when the sun's lower. It'll be fine. As long as we're through, and Papa can do the watering before it gets dark."

A few minutes later, pleased to have Mama's approval, we set out. Rob was sitting in the shade next to his barn. Without a nod or a smile, he watched us go by. He and Tobias were mending tack while Tobias's wife sat nearby with her two-week-old infant clutched in her arms.

"Oh, let's stop and see the baby," Eliza suggested.

"No," Jewel said.

"It's not far," Eliza cajoled, "and it is on our way to the pond."

"No," Jewel repeated.

"Don't you like babies?" Eliza asked.

"No," she answered, looking as if she were about to throw a fit.

Disaster was avoided only because my sister was quick-witted enough to offer the child a piggyback ride. After a moment, though, I had to relieve Eliza, because carrying Jewel made my sister short of breath.

We never got a close-up look at the baby, but we got to the pond and found that Eliza had been wrong. There

wasn't a trace of breeze off the water. Even at the shady
end, the air was thick and stifling.

Both Eliza and Jewel were out-of-sorts yet too tired to
drag themselves back uphill toward our house. Just then,
I didn't give a tinker's dam about either of them.

"I'm not going anywhere," I declared. "And anyone who
wants to be a crybaby can just cry."

I'd no sooner spoken than Jewel's eyes filled with tears.
To my surprise, she didn't howl, she simply collapsed in
a heap and began to shake with silent sobs.

"Do something," I told my sister.

"You do something," she snapped. "Some mother you're
going to make!"

"Shut up," I said.

"You shut up yourself!"

"Make me!"

It was foolish. But before I knew it, Eliza and I were
wrestling, pulling hair, scratching like a pair of wildcats. I
shook Eliza by her shoulders. She responded by stamping
on my foot.

"You're terrible to Cousin Anson," my sister cried.

"Well, you're terrible to Mama," I said. "And to Papa.
I'm tired of doing all the work. Tired of—"

I wanted to rake my nails down her face, but I didn't.
Instead, I twisted one arm behind her back. She surprised
me by jerking away and beginning to attack again.

The fact that the high temperatures had made ours rise
is not startling, yet as we scuffled and scrambled, I realized that I'd never had an honest-to-goodness fight with
my sister. But it felt good, even when we stumbled, fully
clothed, into the water lilies at the shallow end of the pond.

Somehow one thing led to another. Soon we weren't fighting in earnest anymore—just splashing each other with water in mock vengeance.

Jewel, astonished, struggled to her feet, and begged to join in. "The water's free," I told her breathlessly. "If you want to splash, go ahead."

"But Granny Tanner won't be pleased."

"Let Granny Tanner go suck lemons," I declared.

"Oh, Nell," my sister giggled. "Don't—you can't."

"But I can," I insisted. Before my sister could protest, I'd removed every stitch of Jewel's clothes and led her into the water.

"The bottom's icky," she whined.

"Then stay out and be hot."

Pursing her lips together, she waded deeper.

"Watch her," Eliza cautioned. "She probably can't swim!"

What we did next was only one step more ridiculous than what we'd done before. We peeled off our wet stockings and boots. Then, impulsively, I disrobed and immersed myself in the pond.

For a moment, my sister stared in open-mouthed awe.

I smiled. "I'm supposed to look after Jewel, aren't I?"

"Nell, are you soft in the head? This is madness." Yet, even as she spoke, she, too, was stripping and ducking into the water.

No sooner were we in than we wanted to be out. The water was freezing. Although the water lilies and the stand of cattails gave us some protection, we couldn't risk staying there unless we squatted, submerged up to our shoulders. Jewel didn't seem to mind, but Eliza and I began to quiver and shake. That's what we were doing when Anson Tanner found us.

"I came for Jewel," he called, oblivious for the moment to the fact that we were unclothed.

"Do s-s-something," Eliza hissed.

"What?" I asked, taking Jewel in my arms, and backing further into the sheltering green stalks.

Anson Tanner had taken off his suit coat, and I could see rings of sweat under his arms. His eyes were averted from us, and his face wore an odd expression. I couldn't tell if he was horrified or if he wished to unclothe himself and join us in the pond.

"Pappy, I'm in the water," Jewel called.

By now Eliza and I were shivering desperately. Soon, despite Anson Tanner's presence, we'd have to burst from the water and dive for our clothing.

Just then Eliza raised her voice and began to give orders. "Hurry! Run! Go back to the h-h-house!" she told Anson Tanner. "Get a towel! Jewel needs a towel!"

Without a word, Anson Tanner wheeled and strode off uphill in the direction of our farm. Relieved, we fled from the water and scrambled for our clothes. Jewel, not making a move to help herself, stood there watching us.

"Oh, thank you, thank you," I told Eliza. "You saved me. Another minute and he'd have seen me without clothes on!"

Eliza clutched at the front of her unbuttoned dress. "You?" she said incredulously. "He'd have seen *you?* It's *me* he might have seen. He'll see *you* bare soon enough!"

Bare? Without clothes on? But will he? Could I possibly allow that?

Tuesday, July 4, 1899

This morning, all the church bells rang out because it was Independence Day. Independence Day may mean freedom and parades to men, but it has minimal significance to women. Otherwise, Mama, Eliza, and I would not have been imprisoned in the kitchen putting up tomatoes. But Mama said that tomatoes have never learned to read a calendar, and if they're ripe, they're ripe. According to her, we should have been relieved that it'd cooled off a bit.

Eliza wasn't relieved. She was pouty. She said she'd be prostrate before we rode to Hadley this afternoon. We were going there with Anson Tanner and his family to see a traveling circus. Eliza said the circus would be dreadful, especially since the kitchen was sapping her strength and making her hair frizz.

To blot out her complaints, I daydreamed about my quilt as I scalded and skinned tomatoes. I have two blocks nearly completed. Yesterday I stitched red strawberries on a swatch of black satin. I also put a twig of ripe peaches onto gray faille, and a horseshoe on a square of cinnamon silk.

Eliza says my peaches look like little babies' bottoms with leaves, and she says I should use some of the ready-made patterns in Grandmother's basket. She thinks they would add more glamour to the quilt. I am ignoring her suggestions, because this is my work and I shall embroider it as I see fit.

The embroidery is making me more tranquil than anything else I'm doing these days. It helps me conserve energy, too, since I continue to eat sparingly. My constitution has changed. Now, if I overeat, my system rebels, cramping up and rendering me altogether miserable.

Being abstemious is the way to keep myself healthy. It's easier to eradicate images of food if, when I sew, I imagine Grandmother clothed in the navy plaid when she marched for better conditions for millworkers. Instead of dwelling on corn bread and bacon, on plum pie or maple sugar, I stitch a calla lily on black velvet and wonder if that's what Grandmother wore to evening meetings where she spoke about health clinics for the poor.

No one in my family cares about these suppositions of mine. Nor does Rob. Last week, he accosted me on the front porch and made scathing remarks when I tried to talk about Grandmother Shaw. He said my interest in her and in my quiltwork is a kind of madness. I shrugged him off. Rob is becoming increasingly peripheral to my life, and my family is encouraging this alienation. Papa says that now that I am affianced, carousing like a hoyden is unseemly. I know he's right. But sometimes I'm lonely for the days when Rob and I were at ease with one another. That's why I wasn't displeased when Mama discovered we were going to be two jars short for our tomatoes.

"I'll run to the Hoffmans' and borrow them," I told her.

Then, before Eliza could vie for the privilege of escaping from the kitchen, I trotted off, leaving her to help Mama ladle scalding tomatoes from the vat to the rows of glass jars.

When Mrs. Hoffman gave me the jars, I knew I should head straight home, but I dawdled until I managed to find

Rob in the lean-to grape arbor on the south side of the house.

"What are you doing?" I asked.

"Tying up grapes," he replied. "How come you're not sewing? How come they let you out?"

I shrugged. "Time off for good behavior, I guess."

Once Rob would have laughed at my comment, but today he glowered.

"Rob?" I said, stepping into the dappled shade of the arbor.

He wrapped a length of twine around a sagging vine. "What?"

"Did I tell you that I embroidered your initials on one patch of my quilt? RTH. In yellow. Fancy letters with sprays of wheat behind them."

"You never tell me anything anymore."

"Talk to me, Rob. Please . . ."

"Why? Because, after weeks of sending me to Coventry, you show up?"

I hunkered closer to the side of his house. "I'm sorry. I've treated you wretchedly. Forgive me. Please. For all of it. Can't we start over? I'm the same. You're the same."

Rob shook his head. "That's not true. You look and act like a different person. And for some reason you're whittling yourself down to the size of a peppermint stick, fixing to marry a man you don't even care for."

"But I do care for him," I said. "And for Jewel as well. You've seen me looking after her, haven't you?"

"Yes, sometimes. If you can't get Eliza to do it for you. And what are you going to do when you're married? Take Eliza along to mind her?"

Rob cut the twine with his knife. Then he began to secure another loop of vine.

"It's a waste," he insisted.

His words irritated me. I'd tried to apologize and have a pleasant conversation.

"So I'm a waste, am I? Well, what about you? Rob the Adventurer. Rob who was going off to sea or to be a hero. What are you doing? Mending tack and tying up grapes. If that's not a waste, what is? Why isn't Tobias doing this work instead of you? Why? How come?"

"Because his baby died last night," Rob said. "And because his wife is doing poorly."

"The baby's dead?"

Rob nodded. "Yes. Fever, I think. Only the women know, and they don't discuss it in front of me. But maybe you should find out, Nell. Take note before the same thing happens to you!"

"Stop!" I cried. "Don't talk that way. Since when are you so cruel?"

"I'm not being any crueler to you than you're being to yourself."

The glass jars clattered as I clutched them against my chest. "You are. And if I seem like a stranger, you seem like one, too. The next thing I know, you'll give in to your folks and start college."

"They're encouraging me. But I don't think I'll do it."

He was lying, and his words sliced through me like knives. Rob had lied to me all along. He *was* going to go to college. In the fall, when he was lucky enough to be there, I'd be getting married to Anson Tanner.

"Traitor! Rat!"

"Don't, Nell," Rob pleaded, dropping his twine and shears. "Please . . . Don't you see?"

"See what?" I snapped, backing away.

"I'm worried about *you*."

"About me? Why, just look, I'm in rare form. So go on—leave. Go to college. Join the army—whatever. It won't make a whit of difference in my life!"

"You don't see anything, do you?" Rob asked, edging toward me.

I didn't like him getting so close. What was he going to do? Hit me for being so foul-tempered?

"I'm only staying here, Nell, because I'm worried about *you*. Even if you don't want to be with me, how can I desert you when you're not well?"

"Not well? I've never been better in my life. So you might as well go. Run away. Or we could both run away. I think I won't marry Anson Tanner, after all. Maybe when you leave, I'll come with you."

"Come with me?"

I licked my lips. "Why not?"

"Come with me—as *what?*"

"As your friend," I told him. "Maybe we could go to sea together."

Beads of perspiration began to ooze from Rob's brow. "But, Nell, you can't go along with me! This is no dare. It's not possible. It isn't done. Girls like you don't run off. They don't—"

"Why not? Who says it isn't done? Is it better for a girl like me to stay here and get married? Is that what I'm supposed to do? Or not marry and wait? Wait and wait here alone. Is that what you're saying? Is it? Answer me. Answer!"

"Nell, Nellie . . . stop," Rob whispered. "You're not yourself."

This was unbearable. Rob didn't understand. I was fine. Everything was fine. Except for him. Tears in my eyes, I wheeled around, but I collided with someone standing behind me. It was Tobias. How long had he been there? What did he want?

I pulled back abruptly. I stumbled. The glass jars shattered at my feet. Without looking at either Rob or Tobias, I ran back toward the house.

Sitting in the carriage watching elephants parade down the main street of Hadley was like some bizarre nightmare. The church bells were ringing there, too. I couldn't reconcile the elephants, the clowns, the acrobats with what was happening around me.

Tobias's baby was dead, and I was at a circus. One minute I was sewing on a quilt or putting up tomatoes, then the next I was taking Anson Tanner's gloved hand and sitting under a parasol in his four-seater. Only the unwinking sun overhead connected one series of events with another.

Perhaps, like Sleeping Beauty, I'd fallen into a hundred years' slumber. Maybe I was enchanted and the events flowing through my life were imaginings as I awaited the kiss of the prince. But Anson Tanner is the only prince I know. Even if we seldom exchange more than a few dribs and drabs of conversation, he treats me with gallantry. And his kiss will come soon enough.

What about Tobias's wife? Was Tobias *her* prince? And how does Rob fit in? Is he a prince and, if so, whose? Mine? Once, I'd have said yes. But not after hearing him today. The natural order of things seemed suspended.

No one except Anson Tanner is entirely predictable. At the circus parade, his behavior toward me was as unimpeachable as ever, but his mother's confused me. Once we dismounted from the carriage, she kept offering me peanuts to feed to the elephants. I thought they were meant for Jewel, but Jewel had her own sack.

At first, I assumed she wanted me to eat the peanuts myself, because she believed I needed the nourishment. I didn't, of course. I was full, because at dinner I'd had a large cup of corn chowder and a chicken wing.

Only when Mrs. Tanner put one arm about Eliza's shoulder and the other about her son's did I realize that, because of our wide-brimmed straw bonnets, she had confused me with my sister. She thought *I* was the younger sister. She didn't see me as big, strong Nell, but as little Eliza.

What a strange mistake! I should have restrained myself, but I began to laugh. Papa, urged on by Mama, came forward and pulled me aside. His frown told me that he felt my laughter was inappropriate.

"Nell, Nell, my girl, take it easy. Are you having a heat stroke?"

"No, Papa," I whispered. "Mrs. Tanner thinks I'm Liza. She wants me to feed peanuts to the elephants! Because of Jewel, don't you see, because Jewel is crying at the clowns and it is Eliza who is comforting her."

"Don't, Nell, control yourself. Mrs. Tanner's not young, and you've got to be charitable if she gets confused."

"Confused? Maybe she's not. Maybe I *am* Eliza. I'm wearing her frock, and she's in mine. Don't you see how funny this is? Rob would see. Or Rob *would have seen.*"

I was laughing, but I was crying, too. I didn't want to be in Hadley at a circus. I longed to be home sewing on my quilt, home where I was safe. There I would shut myself in my room, and I would stitch a bell, a wreath or—perhaps—an infant's cradle.

Sunday, July 30, 1899

Today in church, our new minister quoted one of his famous Unitarian predecessors, Ralph Waldo Emerson. The sermon was an elaboration of Emerson's statement: "The only gift is a portion of thyself." Sitting there, I felt the words being etched into my head, since it often seems these days as if I am being gifted to Anson Tanner, in a way which demands an unreasonably large part of me.

This morning my gift was my presence in the Tanner family pew. For the occasion, Mama had dressed me in a newly altered red-checked frock and a rose-trimmed bonnet. Papa was with me, but Mama and Eliza were home preparing dinner for us and for the Tanner family. Jewel, after she'd fingered and sniffed the roses on my head, behaved angelically. She folded her hands, crossed her chickeny ankles, and stared at the pulpit. Once or twice she stirred and pulled at an earlobe, but then she'd settled back into attentiveness.

I wish my conduct had been as exemplary. The more I tried to determine what size portion of myself I could afford to give away, the harder the pew seemed. I twisted and turned, slid forward and backward in search of an elusive bit of comfort. The service was not over a moment too soon, and I was glad to be out in the air again.

"Your quilt's coming on rather well," Papa said, as we drove along Pleasant Street toward the railroad tracks.

It was. In the last few days, I'd embroidered a stand of cattails on white satin, a washbowl on pale pink, and a large lovely patch of forget-me-nots. Each block, I'd decided, would represent someone whose life touched mine.

Rob's, for instance, has his initials, a spaniel, a pair of butterflies, and the forget-me-nots. Grandmother Shaw's has two teapots, the initial of her first name, the horseshoe, a fan, and a columbine. Mama's has a pair of crossed hairpins, lilies of the valley, and a golden key. For Papa, I'm doing an owl in Kensington stitch and a star. When I'm finished, there will also be blocks for Eliza, Anson Tanner, Jewel, Mrs. Tanner, and—of course—myself.

"You're not sorry, are you?" Papa asked, as we headed out of town.

"About the quilt?" I asked, unsure of what we'd just been discussing.

"No, Nellie, about marrying."

We were sitting side by side, and I didn't have to look at him. "Well . . ." I began. I needed to stall and search for the proper response. "I might have preferred to go to college. But this will be better. Now, when I'm gone, you'll be able to hire someone to help Mama. Tobias's wife maybe. Or an immigrant girl."

"Oh, Nell . . . no. We haven't a dime to spare. Even in a good year, we couldn't have sent you to college. And, as for hiring someone to help your mother, it's quite impossible."

"But why? When I've left, you'll have *my* food money and clothing money to spend."

Papa shook his head. "No, it won't work that way. We're already in debt. I may need to borrow from Anson just to keep our heads above water."

I didn't want to hear any more. I was sacrificing my life without improving Mama's. But I had no choice. My parents needed me. Badly. Because I was the collateral for Papa's loan.

Despite persistent waves of despondency, I forced myself to help Mama with the last-minute dinner preparations. We were having chicken, dumplings, soda biscuits, fresh-shelled peas, and gravy. For dessert, there was a peach pie that Eliza had made. Anson Tanner was impressed. I was, too, since my sister didn't usually make any kind of pie.

The dinner was a heavy one, and I only sampled it; but no one seemed to notice, especially after Jewel spilled grape juice over me. Although I tried to pretend I didn't care, I could feel a stiffness in my face. The grape juice would never come out. My red-and-white dress was ruined, and it was—just now—the only garment that fit. I'd been rather vain about it.

After dinner, Eliza and Mama did the washing up while Papa and I sat on the front porch with the Tanners. Papa and Anson Tanner talked about high taxes and how lack of rain was endangering the crops. Anson Tanner said if the drought continues and farmers in our area don't do well his business will suffer, too.

When the dishes were done, Mrs. Tanner and Mama discussed recipes for salted corn and baked beans, while

Eliza played checkers with Jewel and I worked on my quilt. Using ocher velvet, I fashioned a pumpkin appliqué and began to stuff it with leftover scraps of black silk.

Later, after Jewel had fallen asleep on the porch swing, Anson Tanner asked if I would take a walk with him. Begrudgingly, I put aside my unfinished pumpkin and rose to my feet. As we stepped from the porch, I was amused to realize that Mama was restraining Eliza, whispering to her. I couldn't hear the words, but I was sure my sister was being told that she ought to leave us alone. As far as I was concerned, I'd have rather had her with us—between us, even, if that's where she wanted to be.

"I'm sorry about your frock," Anson Tanner said as we strolled off.

His words made me look down. I hadn't bothered to change it. I felt young and foolish, strolling with my fiancé in a dress with grape juice staining the front, but he didn't seem to mind. In fact, to my amazement, he said something rather charming. "You've changed in the last half year, Nell. You look somewhat frailer, but you do have a strong spirit and a joy about you."

Not knowing what to say, I remained silent.

After a moment, he continued. "Don't lose these things. They're gifts from the heavens. Teach them to Jewel and, if you will, to me."

I was so moved by his words that I didn't protest when he reached for my hand. If this was the only gift required of me, I'd be fine. The hand which held mine was dry. Its clasp was gentle. When I looked up, self-conscious to be walking this way, I caught sight of Rob. With the spaniel at his heels and a rifle over his shoulder, he was tromping off toward the woods.

In silence, Anson Tanner and I walked into the orchard. The peaches and plums were finished and the apples were not yet ripe. I wanted to free my hand, yet I didn't wish to be rude. I took a deep breath. Time seemed to be pleasantly suspended.

Then, all of a sudden, a series of high-pitched shrieks pierced the air. The sounds were coming from the cabin Tobias shared with his wife. Startled, I loosened my hand and began to run in that direction. Anson Tanner followed at my heels. But before we could do anything, Rob's father appeared and began to pound on the door. As we stood watching, Tobias opened it. From within, the screams continued, but at a lower pitch. The two men talked. After some nodding of heads, Tobias went back in the cabin and closed the door behind him.

Tobias's wife continued to cry, but less forcefully. I could see her, leaning one shoulder against the front window. As I watched her, Mr. Hoffman came over to us. "I'm sorry for the disturbance," he said. "She's lost her baby, you see, and it's been hard."

"Yes, I know," Anson Tanner replied. "Bearing such losses is difficult."

He turned as if he expected me to speak, as if he hoped he could retrieve my hand and resume our stroll. But I didn't say anything. Nor did I offer my hand.

The day had turned sour. Tobias's wife looked desperate. Sometimes I was, too. Like now, for instance. My knees felt ropy, and my tongue was thick. A downward glance reminded me that my frock appeared to be marked with dried blood.

Then I remembered this morning's sermon. I wasn't sure I agreed with Mr. Emerson. Tobias's wife may be giving too large a portion of herself away. Mama does it, too. That's why she's always so tired. And when I marry, it will happen to me. Anson Tanner will touch me on my hand or wherever he pleases whether I want him to or not. And Jewel will keep turning things over in my lap.

As I was struggling to regain my self-possession, a commotion broke out in our yard. The rooster had escaped again. To my amazement, Eliza ran from the porch and began flapping her arms, chasing the terrible bird so Papa could grab him by the neck and force him back into his pen. Both Jewel and Anson Tanner loved the spectacle. While they applauded, I took my quilt basket from the porch and disappeared into the house.

Later that night, after the Tanners left, Mama produced a bolt of Chinese damask in pure white and a bolt of pale peach silk. "For your wedding, Nell," she whispered. "The last of Grandmother's fabrics."

Before I knew what Mama was doing, she'd spread out a sheet and pulled me to the center of the room. Then, sighing contentedly, she began to unwrap the bolt, draping the fabric about my shoulders and hips.

"This is for you, and the peach is for Liza. There's enough of the peach for Jewel to have a frock, too."

I stood there dumbly. October 28 had always seemed far away. Now that these fabrics had appeared, it seemed closer and more real.

While I gritted my teeth, Eliza began to dance around me, fingering the brocade. "Smile, smile," she said. "You're supposed to look like a bride, not like a wraith."

"Stop," I cried. "No. I don't want to do this now."

Mama rocked back on her heels. "Are you feverish?" she asked.

Papa glanced up over his magazine. He looked concerned.

Mama did, too. "Come on, Nellie, let's unwind this. We can do it when you haven't had such a full day. Maybe you should sit quietly tonight and work on your quilt."

I was angry at them. At all of them, but pleased to find myself coddled for once, I allowed Mama to unwrap the fabric and seat me in the rocking chair with an afghan and a quilt block in my lap. As I resumed work on my velvet pumpkin, she brought me camomile tea and biscuits.

While I sewed and sipped the tea, I was only mildly surprised to see Eliza out in the hallway primping before the glass. Shifting her weight from one foot to the other, she propped the peach silk beneath her chin. When that began to bore her, she dropped it and swathed herself in the shiny brocade.

Wednesday, August 23, 1899

Tuesday night, I couldn't sleep. No matter what position I assumed, the mattress springs pressed against my hips and spine. Of late, many nights are like this. If I manage to drift off, I find myself jolted into wakefulness by the phantom smell of fresh-baked bread or by visions of banquet tables laden with food.

When I could stand it no longer, I got out of bed, lit a candle, and made my way toward the kitchen. I was careful to be quiet, since I didn't want Mama to appear and ask what was wrong.

I was hungry, but instead of giving in to this weakness immediately, I spread a slice of oatmeal bread with butter and laid it upon the sideboard. Then I fetched the basket of quilt blocks and began to work. Last Sunday, I'd learned a new technique—the plush stitch. I was using it to make an ivory-and-buff dahlia to decorate the center of Mrs. Tanner's block. Plush stitch is akin to rug making. It requires two kinds of thread and a shears with which to clip it.

The longer I sat, the cooler the kitchen became. I had to put more coal into the stove and pull my stool closer. The buttered bread smelled good, but my stomach was so knotted with tension over the quality of my stitches and over images of a white brocade wedding gown that I no longer craved it.

Too restless to continue sewing, I opened the kitchen door and slipped outside. The sky was overcast, revealing only a crevice of bluish light where the sun usually rose. I crossed the yard and wandered into the barn. The pigs, curled together like a litter of overlarge kittens, were sound asleep. The cow's eyes were half open, and she lay in her stall, nodding her head soporifically.

Only Papa's horses were awake. The bay and the roan stamped their feet and tossed their heads as I approached. Bending down, I scooped up a handful of hay and offered some to each animal. The two beasts began to chomp on it, exposing rows of huge yellowed teeth.

Their chewing noises made me queasy, so I headed back outside. Thunderclaps had begun to echo from the other side of the valley and I lingered in the yard, listening. After a while, with no particular purpose in mind, I started toward the orchard.

At this time of year, its trees are so heavy with ripening apples that the branches must be propped with Y-shaped stakes. Suddenly, one of those stakes creaked and wobbled in an unnatural manner. For a moment, I was alarmed. Then, between the tree trunks, I caught sight of a grinning red fox.

"I wager I can stay stiller than you," I told him.

I was wrong. The ground beneath my feet was so cold that my body started to shiver. While the fox remained motionless as a dead thing, I had to stamp my feet. When I moved, he vanished into the woods beyond the orchard.

"Warm up, warm up," I told myself. I could have gone back indoors and huddled by the stove again, but being here when everyone else was asleep was exhilarating.

The woods and fields, the pond and river were lit by intermittent flares of lightning. How astonishingly lovely the world could be. Watching and listening, I found myself singing aloud.

Mine eyes have seen . . .
Of the coming of the Lord.
He hath trampled out . . .
Where the . . .

My voice was swallowed by the sound of the mounting wind. But I didn't care. I was singing for myself. Well, perhaps a part of me was singing for my family and for Anson Tanner.

Slowly, I began to spin in circles, making my gown billow about my ankles. I spun and spun. I was dizzy, very dizzy, when something caught my eye—a few weathered boards in a crotch of one of our oldest trees. It was the remnants of a tree house where Rob and I had played when we were smaller.

On an impulse, I began to hitch myself up to that platform. To facilitate the climb, I twisted my gown about my hips. I knew I was lighter than I'd been in years, but my body seemed heavy and sluggish.

For a moment, I regretted having left the bread and butter on the sideboard. Then I dismissed the thought. If I was truly hungry, I was surrounded by apples. As the trunk swayed from my weight, some of them dropped to the ground. Papa would be dismayed at the waste.

"A pity," I told myself. "But this storm will shake loose more than that."

My words were hardly out when lightning with a simultaneous crack of thunder struck beyond the nearest ridge of hills. Overtired from such exertion, I was not disturbed that the storm was about to engulf me. Reaching up, I grabbed for a bough above the old platform. With one hand I grasped it, then with the other. For a moment I swung there. Next, arching my body in a way I remembered, I bent my knees and lunged forward to land on the planking.

I was there. Yet, as I was trying to get my balance, another bolt of lightning startled me. My hands slipped, and I dropped heavily onto the platform. Before I could make any move to steady myself, the rotted boards split, more apples fell to the ground, and I did, too.

I was stunned but conscious when I heard footsteps. At first, I assumed it was Papa, but the footsteps were lighter than his and more tentative. As the man came up behind me, I thought I heard a horse whinny. I lay there, eyes closed, unmoving while the man knelt and lifted me in his arms. My body ached, and my head also. The man's chin rested against my forehead. Whoever it was, he was clean-shaven, and Papa wore a beard. Besides, this man didn't smell of tobacco.

Perhaps it was Anson Tanner, who'd ridden out in the storm to see if I was all right. With some kind of psychic perception, he'd come to check on my welfare. At this moment, the white brocade didn't seem so threatening.

I heard the horse again, also more wind and thunder-bolts. Rain was beginning to fall in sheets. Anson, instead of heading for the house, carried me to the stable. Once inside, he lowered us both onto the hay pile from which the stock was fed. I was sleepy. After an endless night, what I really wanted to do was sleep right where I was.

I could hear the violence of the storm, but I was re-laxed. Wind and rain battered the barn. The animals shifted nervously in their stalls. When I pressed my face against the dark, rough cloth of his shirt, I smelled perspiration, and something niggled at me. Something about a horse. Had Anson Tanner left his horse out in such a storm? Would he have been that careless?

No. Absolutely not. This was all wrong. I opened my eyes and struggled to make the world come back into fo-cus. There'd been no horse outside—only inside the barn. One of our own horses. And it wasn't Anson Tanner who'd rescued me from the orchard. It was Tobias.

Horrified, I wrenched free of his grasp and staggered to my feet. Faint, struggling to retain consciousness, I stepped backwards. Then, dipping my hands into a bin of manure, I began to fling one clod after another in his direction.

Thursday, August 31, 1899

I couldn't tell anyone about Tobias, since the encounter with him had been my own fault. But I was more careful. After the night of the storm, I seldom went anywhere unaccompanied. Despite my persistent moodiness, I've attempted to be as obedient as possible. It's been a strain, though, since I've had little incentive to do anything except sew on my quilt.

I've just finished an embroidered row of amaryllis and a pieced fan. Now I'm copying one of Grandmother Shaw's porcelain figures—a girl in a hat and apron. She's stiff and hard and shiny. Her shoulders droop as if she's bearing the weight of the world. I'm rendering her from the back, because from that angle I think she looks like me. She'll be part of my block, standing to the left of my name.

Eliza has begun to complain that I'm spending an inordinate amount of time on my quilt. I'm horrid, she says, making so much work for her that she hasn't time to visit with school friends or trade romance novels with them. I don't answer, except to say that the quilt must be finished before October 28. Eliza didn't mind when I labored over it in the evenings, but she's provoked when she finds me spending half the day piecing and stitching on the front porch.

Eliza's been assisting Mama with most of the garden work and summer preserving. These are hot, thankless tasks. After last week's storm stripped our plantings, there's been an extra rush to get the corn salted down and the windfall apples dried.

Papa is moody about the crop loss. He says the wolf's at our door, that we'll be hard-pressed this winter. He's so worried he's decided to butcher one of our hogs. Ordinarily, we don't do this until the first cold spell in November. Now it's necessary because we must barter most of it for grain and other supplies needed to tide us through the winter.

Today, while the men—Papa had asked Rob, Tobias, and Mr. Hoffman in to help with the hog slaughter—were behind the barn attending to their grisly job, I had a good excuse to keep from working. Mama had cut the muslin pattern for my bridal gown and wanted to fit it on me.

Eliza and Jewel, who was visiting for the day, were left in charge of turning the apple rings that lay upon the drying screens in the yard. The two of them had to stay there in the sun to keep birds from pecking at the apples.

While Mama waited in the parlor, I went upstairs to put on the muslin. It was too big. My mother would not be pleased. My body continues to whittle itself down. I have hipbones I haven't seen since I was nine, and my backbone's protruding like a rope of oversize pearls. To make certain Mama didn't see this, I donned a pair of starched chemises and several petticoats. Then, before I descended, I drank a full pitcher of water.

Mama clucked as she nipped in the pattern, but she chose to comment on my attitude instead of on my size. "You've been skittish," she said. "Frightened, I suppose. Every bride gets the jitters. But you'll be all right, Nellie. Really you will."

"I'm not sure," I told her.

"You don't have to marry."

"But I do. I promised."

"Nell, wait—listen. Why don't we sit down and talk?"

"There's nothing to talk about. Go on with the fitting."

Averting her eyes, Mama tugged at the muslin. "Whatever you like. Shall we discuss your gown? I hope you'll approve. I've chosen a Butterick pattern with a flounce and a train. One side will be pulled up with a ribbon. And Liza's will be the same. Jewel's frock—the Tanners' housekeeper will do it—will be simple, with a pinafore to go over it."

Mama tried to solicit my opinions about these matters, but my mind floated from one dark image to another. These images were the kind that haunted me when I was in bed at night. Little by little, my food dreams were being blotted out by images of inky flying things with leering faces. Now, even in daylight, they pinched and pulled at me, until finally I wobbled, stumbling away from my mother.

"What's wrong?" she asked.

"Nothing," I told her.

"You missed breakfast again this morning. Maybe you should have some porridge. There's fresh corn bread, too."

"I ate before anyone was up," I said, cupping my hands over my water-filled belly. "Look how full my stomach is."

My words didn't satisfy her, but she chose not to pursue the subject. When the fitting was over and I had changed, she asked me to help with dinner. We fixed cucumbers, chicken, and corn bread with apple butter. None of it appealed to me. I volunteered to watch over the apple commands, grunts, no one seemed to have heard the cry except me.

A second cry followed the first one. I jumped to my feet. It was Jewel. And where was Eliza? Had my sister left her unattended? Or had Eliza asked me to watch her, and had I been oblivious? My heart in my throat, I dashed off toward the privy.

Was Jewel alone? Or was someone else with her?

In half a minute, I was down by the privy. Shaking, I grabbed at the door. It rattled, but it wouldn't budge.

"Open it, open it!" I shouted, throwing my weight against it. "Open it!"

My vision of what I'd find within was so awful I was tempted to turn tail and run off. But I didn't. Instead, I heaved one shoulder against the door and pushed until I ripped the hook from the porous old pine.

And there was Jewel. She was alone. But, I asked myself, had Tobias been hanging around? Had he frightened her so much that she'd had to lock herself in?

I fell to my knees and took hold of her. She smelled foul. Before I could begin to question her, however, she began to babble.

"I couldn't. It was too dirty, too high, too dark. At home we have a toilet, at home . . ."

She'd soiled herself and cried out in humiliation. And it hadn't been her fault. Not Tobias's, either. But mine, for ignoring her.

Holding such a nasty-smelling creature against my body was repellent, but I did make an attempt to comfort her. Next, handling her gingerly, I took her off to the kitchen. There, I dragged out the zinc bathing tub and filled it with a mixture of hot water from the stove's reservoir and cold from the kitchen tap. Then I stripped off her clothes and lowered her into the tub.

That's where she was when Eliza, weighted down by a bucket of pig entrails, came into the kitchen.

"Look after her," I told my sister.

A grimace indicated that Eliza did not like either my tone or my words. "But I'm busy. I've covered the apples, and now I'm helping with the slaughter."

"I don't care," I said.

"What's she doing in the tub? Since when do we give her baths?"

As Eliza and I squabbled, Jewel huddled in the lukewarm water, looking miserable.

"I'm unable to cope with this," I said, speaking half to Eliza and half to Jewel.

"But you're going to be her *mother*!" Eliza said, setting down the pail of guts and kneeling beside the child.

"Maybe yes. Maybe no," I muttered through clenched teeth. "But right now I'm not. Right now I feel sick and I'm going upstairs to lie down."

Without another word, I abandoned them both, walking slowly through the house, up the stairs, toward my room and my bed.

Friday, September 15, 1899

Mama thinks I am sick, but she's wrong. I'm not sick at all. She insists that I'm dyspeptic, that I've gone into a woman in the brown striped gingham who served us tea and scones than like Mrs. Tanner. I could not see myself spending days sitting beside her laboring over tedious ornamental work. Once my quilt was finished, I did not plan to take up a needle and thread again, except perhaps to sew on a button or fix a hem.

"Eat another scone," Mrs. Tanner urged me, unaware that I'd smuggled the first one into my pocket. "Put jam on it, too."

Then, as if I weren't even in the room, she turned to Mama and said, "Has Nellie been ill? I may be old as white thread, but it looks as if she needs to put more meat on her bones."

Mama smiled nervously and began to describe the progress being made on my wedding gown. It was obvious that she didn't intend to discuss my health or mention our visit to Dr. Sternhagen. As they talked, Papa puffed on his pipe. His face was blank. I hoped mine was, too.

As Mama and Mrs. Tanner discussed my dress, the Unity Church, and the reception to be held at our home afterward, Jewel dropped her embroidery hoop and came over next to my chair. She didn't say anything. She just stood there with a snotty nose, which she made no attempt to wipe.

"Jewel," Mrs. Tanner called out. "Where's your hanky? Use it. And mind your manners. Staring is impolite."

Hunching her shoulders, Jewel fished in the pocket of her pinafore until she found a linen square with lace edging. She swabbed at her face, spreading green slime across one cheek.

Feeling an unexpected surge of emotion, I took hold of

the handkerchief and wiped her face. Then I held the hanky beneath her nose in a way I remember Mama doing for me.

"Blow," I said.

As Jewel obeyed, a faint smile skittered across her face. All of a sudden, I felt tender and loving. It was perplexing to me how I could be detached and disagreeable one moment and the next be fond of the child.

But then she destroyed my maternal instincts by making an unwelcome observation. "Why did you put that scone in your pocket?"

Startled, I glanced about to see if anyone else had heard her words. Not Mama or Mrs. Tanner. They were discussing the best way to trim a winter bonnet. Beneath Papa's mustache, the corners of his mouth were tight, but he was not looking at me.

"Why?" Jewel repeated.

"Hush," I told her. Then I lied. "It's so good I want to save it for later. But this is our secret."

Jewel squinched up her eyes. "I do that sometimes, too," she whispered. "But we must not let Granny see, or she'll spank us."

Yes, of course. At that instant, I believed her. When I was married to Anson Tanner, his mother might discipline me in the same manner she disciplined Jewel.

My ordeal with Anson Tanner's daughter was not over, however. Now that she viewed us as co-conspirators, she was more intimate than usual.

"Why are your eyes so blue?" she asked.

I frowned. "They're not. I've got brown eyes."

"Oh, no," she protested. "Not that part—the part *under* your eyes."

Did I have circles under my eyes? Probably so, but it irritated me that Jewel would ask about them. I mumbled some answer about lack of sleep, and then, by turning away, I made sure she knew I had nothing more to say.

When the tortuous visit was over and we were home again, Mama gave me a dose of Dr. Sternhagen's elixir and urged me to follow some of his advice. "Take a walk, Nellie. It should stir your blood and work up an appetite for supper."

I would have preferred to sit on the porch, assembling quilt blocks, but—instead of arguing—I walked out, leaving Mama and Eliza to finish the bread, collect the eggs, and finish the chores we hadn't had time to do in the morning. Although I heard Liza complaining about how pampered I'd become, I didn't turn back or offer to help. Instead, feeling so light I could almost float, I headed toward the orchard.

The late afternoon rays slanted down, making the woods and fields glow with subtle color. In the orchard, ripe apples shone like oversize rubies. After enduring an afternoon in the Tanners' back parlor, I found such beauty particularly welcome.

Drifting along, I inhaled the sharp-sweet smell of apples mingling with the scent of new-cut hay. Rob was in the orchard on our apple-picking ladder, with a heavy basket dangling in the crook of his arm. In exchange for the maple syrup the Hoffmans gave us each year, we gave them a portion of our russets.

For reasons which eluded me, I was pleased to see Rob. I headed toward him. "Hello," I said.

"Hello," he answered tonelessly. After a minute or two, he backed down the ladder and set his basket on the ground.

Then he wiped an apple against the bib of his overalls and took a bite from it.

I wanted to say something nice, tell him how much I'd missed his company during the past four months. But I was ill at ease, oddly shy. We'd exchanged so many bitter words I didn't know how to begin setting things right, and the last time I'd tried to apologize, he'd been angry with me.

He didn't look any happier now. For a long while, as he stood shuffling his feet and chomping on the apple, he stared at me. Then, finally, he spoke. "Nell—don't marry Mr. Tanner. Please. That's what's making you ill."

My good mood had vanished. "It's not your concern," I told him.

"I can't stay around much longer—stay here and see what's happening to you."

"Did I ask you to? Besides, aren't you leaving? Aren't you starting college?"

Before Rob could answer, Tobias's wife appeared at the far end of the orchard. She had a burlap sack over one arm. She'd come to take a few apples for her own table. Not that anyone would care, but she looked frightened that we should see her. Her face was gaunt, her hair lank, and her clothes hung about her shapeless body. Impulsively, I waved in her direction, but the moment I did, she turned and fled.

"Now *that's* someone who's sick," I told Rob. "Why don't you worry about her, instead of about me?"

Rob licked his lips. "I worry about her, too. But you and she aren't so different, Nell. Have you looked at yourself lately?"

I didn't answer. Instead, I turned my back on him and

headed toward the house. Once inside, I went directly upstairs and lay down to rest. Only when sounds from below
assured me supper was over did I venture down. But, to
my dismay, Mama was waiting for me. Again she produced Dr. Sternhagen's bottle of dark, evil-tasting elixir
and dosed me with it. Then she warmed some barley soup
and sat there while I consumed it.

I swallowed slowly, feeling like a child who would be
punished if she didn't finish her meal. Long before Mama
let me leave the table, I was full. I was upset, too, because
eating so much broke my rules about how much food I
was allowed and because, when I was married to Anson
Tanner, his mother would sit beside me to monitor what
I ate.

Afterward, unwillingly, I sat in the parlor with my family. Papa and Eliza played cribbage while Mama helped
me assemble the nine quilt blocks. Sewing them together
should have pleased me because it meant the quilt was
almost done. Instead, it was a vivid reminder that there
were only six weeks until I was to be married.

I felt irritable and unsettled. The quilt had lost its abil-
ity to comfort me. It looked ugly, particularly the center
block where the patched fabrics surrounded a large, empty
diamond of coal black velvet.

Then, as I was brooding, Mama said, "Look here, Nell.
Now you're ready for the best part . . ."

As I watched, she drew paper patterns from the bottom
of the basket and began to explain that the patches were
ready to be edged. I would use my twenty-four colors of
thread and work fancy stitches around each scrap of fabric. Every single patch needed its own decorative border.
What a lot of work!

When Mama started to enumerate the stitches she'd need to teach me, I almost swooned with relief. They sounded so beautiful and so complicated—brier stitch, coral stitch, double cross-stitch, herringbone, catstitch, French knots, featherstitch, point russe, lazy daisy. Stitches, stitches and more stitches. It would take time to learn them, time to do them. And that's what I wanted most of all just now. Time.

Tuesday, September 26, 1899

Mama's pleased with me. She thinks Dr. Sternhagen's elixir is working and my appetite has returned. But she's wrong. As she was kissing Eliza, seeing her off to school this morning, I dumped my oatmeal in the hogs' slop bucket and covered it with cabbage leaves.

I've always hated deceit, but I am becoming clever at it. Although the foul-flavored elixir gives me a sense of well-being, my body continues to require little food. Still, I have renewed energy and vigor. I am taking long walks. I'm embroidering lovely multicolored borders around the patches of my quilt, and I even help with the household tasks again.

This morning's project was soap making. We'd just lit the outside fire and begun to assemble the vats when Anson Tanner, bringing Jewel to spend the day with us, drove his rig into our yard. In his own way, he seemed charmed to find that his daughter was going to discover that soap—

like apples and maple syrup—did not have to come from the store.

"She's flourishing," he said softly. "The farm is good for her. See how she's filling out."

I didn't reply. Jewel was standing pigeon-toed, clutching her father's hand and sucking on a strand of hair. To me, she looked as wizened as ever. Now her narrow face was scrubbed clean and her blue jumper was stiff with starch. Yet, by the time her father came this afternoon, she'd be filthy and disreputable-looking. Not something calculated to endear me to Mrs. Tanner.

"Soap making must be a rewarding activity," Anson Tanner said.

I agreed. The three of us exchanged a few additional pleasantries. Then Mama produced a basket and took Jewel to the henhouse to collect eggs.

Anson Tanner appeared disconcerted to find himself alone with me. He adjusted his gaze so that his eyes focused just above my left shoulder. "You're looking well," he told me.

Smiling self-consciously, I pulled at the end of my braid. My hair felt greasy and in need of a good wash, but the rest of me was padded with extra vests, petticoats. A large apron over my work dress made me even fuller. One of my strictest rules was that only I was to know how tiny I'd become. I was lucky, too, since the day's breeze would keep me from being overwarm.

Because I suspected that Mama would linger in the henhouse with Jewel as long as she possibly could, I was uneasy. I would need more than smiles to get me through this morning's ordeal.

"Could I offer you some refreshment?" I asked, struggling to behave appropriately. He agreed, and soon I found myself at the kitchen table, drinking coffee with him.

"Mother wants you to come this week and go through the linens. She wants you to choose what you want for our portion of the house."

"I know so little about linens," I murmured.

"Don't worry about it," he said. "Mother cares strongly for you, and she'll teach you what you need to know."

The first part of his statement seemed altogether untrue and the second unremittingly accurate. In any case, I did not wish to talk about linens or about his mother. I needed to find another topic of conversation. Was it appropriate to ask about making shoes? What would I say? Ask what styles were selling well or whether his women employees were well treated? Was his shoe factory what we were going to discuss when we were married and sat this way every single morning? I shuddered.

"Are you too cool?" he asked. His sensitivity was reassuring. It made me feel generous toward him—a little giddy, even.

I jumped to my feet. "Come," I urged him. "Come into the parlor. I want you to see my quilt."

The words were no sooner out than I knew I'd said the wrong thing. Was it *my* quilt I was creating, or should I have said it was *ours*? A quilt for *our* home.

Anson Tanner was too taken with my masterpiece to notice this discomfort. "Oh, Nell, it's quite superior," he declared, arranging it over the back of the sofa.

Flushed with his praise, I started to jabber, explaining that the fabrics had come from my Grandmother Shaw, who'd been a campaigner for women's suffrage, that they were scraps from frocks she'd worn.

"Your grandmother must have had an astonishing number of garments," he commented, running a finger from patch to patch.

"Well, some of the fabrics are ours." Because I didn't think I should discuss how prosperous my grandmother had been, I began to show him that the different blocks represented different people.

"Which is mine?" he asked.

I pointed. "This one."

"Quite plain," he commented. "A cattail, a shoe, my initial." But, before I could decide if I'd done him an injustice, he reassured me by saying he *was* a plain person and his block was entirely suitable.

His tact made me feel guilty. So I pointed out something else. "Look, next to your initial. See? That's a scrap from the wedding gown." As soon as the words were out of my mouth, I regretted them.

I snatched up the quilt and tried to stuff it back in its basket. I was sorry I'd let him see it. The crazy quilt was *mine*, and I knew I'd never want to share it with him—no matter how kind and considerate he was.

My behavior didn't disturb him. He looked as if he thought I was conducting myself as any young woman might when left in an unexpectedly intimate situation with her prospective husband. Taking my elbow, he told me that he must be off for work and asked if I'd walk him to his rig. I nodded and let him lead me back outside.

Mama and Jewel, having finished in the henhouse, were back by the fire pit. Mama was pouring Red Devil Lye into the big vat. "Then," she explained to Jewel, "we'll add the old bacon grease and new hog fat."

Even if she seemed to have her attention fixed on Jewel,

I knew she saw Anson Tanner's fingers on my elbow. I wanted to wrench myself free, yet at the same time I wanted him to pull me closer. Instead, he dropped his hand and went to wish Mama goodbye. Next he stooped and gave Jewel a kiss on the cheek.

Trying to regain my composure, I walked him over to his rig. As we stood there, he reached out and lifted up the hand on which I wore his garnet ring. "It's loose," he commented. "I should have it tightened."

Then, before I knew what was happening, he pressed my fingers against his lips. I was stunned. The only thing that kept my head clear was the slight odor of fish that exuded from between his lips.

As soon as he'd driven off, Mama stopped her dallying. Soap making is not particularly hard—especially now that we use store-bought lye instead of making our own—but it's time-consuming, so we needed to get started. Soon we had two vats on the pit and were stirring them, letting the brown gravylike substance thicken over the heat.

When Jewel pleaded to be allowed to stir, Mama refused, afraid the child would burn herself or inhale caustic fumes. Then Jewel, showing a bit of the temperament one might expect from a redhead, began to fuss because she had nothing to do.

"I can stir both kettles," Mama said. "Find the tabby for her to play with. Or walk her to the pasture so she can see the mowing."

Taking Mama's second suggestion, I led Jewel toward the Hoffman pasture, where Papa, Rob, Mr. Hoffman, Tobias, and his wife were at work. Hay mowing was another common activity that we shared with the Hoffmans.

Tobias squinted when he glanced toward me. His wife, looking characteristically grim, knelt on the ground, cutting lengths of cord.

Rob ignored us for a while, but at last he pulled off his work gloves and came over to where we stood. I smiled, pleased to find him making this effort.

Instead of returning my smile, he bent down and took hold of Jewel. Lifting her, he swung her through the air until she began to yelp and squeal to be put down.

He granted her request. As she staggered away, Rob took hold of my arm. "I'm leaving," he said.

"Leaving?"

"Stop acting so barmy, Nell. You make me want to shake you till your teeth rattle."

I pulled my arm loose. "Barmy?" I asked. "Why, I'm my old self."

"Are you?"

"What does that mean?"

"It means, Nell, that if I didn't know you better, I'd swear you'd been drinking."

"What a silly notion. What—"

I never finished my sentence because Jewel, tugging at my skirt, interrupted me. "Stop them. Make them stop!"

I turned but saw nothing that struck me as unusual.

"Make them stop!" Jewel cried again. This time she pointed her finger. "No, no!"

When Rob and I saw what was upsetting Jewel, we reacted in the identical way. We both began to laugh. In the adjoining field, our stallion was mounting the sturdy bay mare. I wanted to explain it to Jewel, but—before I could do a thing—Rob threw his arms around me. Without hesitating, I followed suit. Then, holding onto one another, we hooted and howled. We jumped up and down. For an instant, the last few months fell away, and the two of us were as we had always been—no arguments or misunderstandings between us.

Buoyed up by a surge of happiness, I made a mad suggestion. "Kiss me," I urged Rob. "Anson Tanner kissed my hand. If you're going, if you're leaving, can't you do the same? I dare you!"

Rob's hands dropped to his side. He pushed me away. When he spoke, his voice sounded choked, unnatural. "Kiss you? I couldn't. Not now."

He couldn't? Not now. Why? Disoriented, I grabbed for Jewel's hand and began to run toward the house.

Jewel was crying, but I didn't slow down, because Rob was running, too. He was coming after us, catching up. He grabbed my arm and, pulling me aside, spoke in low, urgent tones. "Nell . . . Nell . . . don't do it. You're killing yourself. Don't marry Anson Tanner. Don't. *I* dare *you!*"

As I stood back at the pit, stirring the thickening vats of soap, Rob's words echoed inside my head. Jewel was sulking on the porch. Mama was readying the flat pans into which we'd pour the mixture. I had nothing to do but stir. The ring was loose on my finger, irritating me as it slipped about.

Images of the morning overlapped. Anson Tanner touching my quilt, my elbow, kissing my hand. The stallion mounting the mare. Jewel crying. Rob holding me, laughing with me. Rob pushing me away. The huskiness in his voice. My dare to Rob, his to me.

Everything, suddenly, seemed so muddled, as opaque

as the soap I was about to pour from the vat. Balancing it carefully, using a piece of flannel to shield my right hand from the heat, I began to dribble the hot brown liquid into the waiting pans.

The kettle was heavy. My arms were weak, as if I needed another dose of Dr. Sternhagen's elixir. My grip on the handle wasn't secure enough. I tried to shift the potholder. As I did, my hand opened, and the garnet ring slipped from my finger. It dropped into the pan of scalding soap.

I could have put down the vat, reached for a spoon, and fished it out. But I didn't. Instead, I kept on pouring. Soon the ring disappeared under layers of soap.

I wasn't worried. I knew where the ring was. Anson Tanner's ring wasn't lost. It was merely hiding. When the soap had hardened, we'd cut it into neat oblongs. Soon, someone in our family—maybe even me—would wash with that particular bar of soap and find deep within it a secret prize.

Wednesday, October 4, 1899

Sometime after midnight a noise startled me—a noise from outside in the yard. I lay in my bed and listened. It sounded like splashing water.

I should have been upset at being awakened, but I hadn't been asleep. I'd been lying there picturing Anson Tanner's ring embedded in yellow-brown soap, thinking of the strange blank black diamond in the center of my quilt. And at the same time I'd been thinking about food—white rice, glistening mashed potatoes, egg bread slathered with butter.

The splashing continued. Slowly, I sat up. I listened. It wasn't rain I was hearing. I knew, because through my bedroom window I could see a star-stippled sky.

The mysterious sound was accompanied by a rhythmic metallic squeak. Rising from my bed, I tiptoed toward the open window. I peered out. Now everything made sense. I'd been hearing our yard pump. Standing next to it, holding its handle, was Rob. He was looking up at my window. When he saw me, he beckoned.

Nodding, I turned and walked from my room, down the stairs, through the kitchen, then out into the yard. The fact that I was barefoot and clothed only in my nightdress seemed unimportant. By the time I was next to the pump, Rob's hand was reaching out for mine.

"Goodbye," he said. On his back, he had a bundle tied up with twine. On his head, he was wearing his old blue cap. "I left. I was all the way to town, but I came back. I couldn't leave without seeing you."

Rob tried to withdraw his hand, but I wouldn't let him. "Don't go," I said.

"I have to. I don't understand what's happened, Nell, or what's happening. All I know is that I must get away."

"Stay—just for an hour," I urged. "We can run down to the pond and skip stones by moonlight. We can go up in the loft and bury ourselves in hay."

"It's too late," Rob told me. "You and I don't do those things anymore."

"It's not too late. No, no—it's not."

"But it is."

"Why?"

"Can't you see? No, I guess you can't. You do for your parents and your sister. Or for Tanner and his little girl. You even take time to worry about Tobias's wife, Ludie. But you've forgotten how to take care of Nell."

It was cold, and I was beginning to shiver. I had no answer for what Rob had just said, so I remained silent.

"Nell, did you hear me? Are you sleepwalking, or are you awake?"

"I'm awake."

Leaning forward, he peered into my eyes. Then he lifted the hand he was holding and examined it. "Where's your ring?"

"In a bar of soap," I said.

"That's a half-witted answer."

"No, it's the truth."

"I don't understand you. I swear I don't. Can't you say anything that makes sense?" he pleaded.

I swallowed. I tilted my head, so that my braid swung back and forth behind my shoulders. Finally I spoke. "Where are you going?"

"I don't know," Rob said.

"Will you write?"

"No."

"Why not?" I asked.

He shifted his weight from one foot to the other. "Because." Abruptly, he released my hand. He took off his cap, and putting down his pack, he ducked his head under the pump and gave the handle another pull. Cold water splashed over his head. It splattered against my bare feet, making me feel colder. I folded my arms across my chest, hugging myself to ward off the chill.

Rob stood up. Rivulets of water ran from his hair down

his face and onto the shoulders of his jacket. I could see his breath and mine rising in pale white clouds before our faces. The clouds merged and mingled, blurring my view of his face, so I couldn't tell if he was looking at me with fondness or with loathing.

Just when I imagined he was about to reach out and pull me close, he bent down and picked up his pack.

I moved toward him, but he backed up.

"Don't leave me," I said.

"I must."

"Rob . . . please. Wait. You can't walk off like this."

"I'm sorry, but that's what I'm going to do."

"Without kissing me goodbye? But it was a dare. I *dared* you!"

"I know," he said with an apologetic shrug. "But I can't."

"Why?"

"Because you're not the same person. Not the old Nell— not *my* Nell. You're different now. Almost like some strange boy in skirts."

Then, turning his back to me, he strode off into the darkness.

"Wait," I cried. "Listen. Wait. If you don't accept my dare, why should I pay attention to yours? You dared me, didn't you? Dared me not to marry Anson Tanner. Aren't you going to stay to see what I do?"

I stood motionlessly, straining for his answer, but he didn't offer one. The sound of his retreating footsteps was the only reply he gave.

Distraught, I stumbled back into the yard. Instead of feeling cold, I was unexpectedly hot, as if my head were on fire. Without pausing to think, I knelt below the pump and yanked at the handle until water began to flow, soaking me, drenching me, cooling me off.

Then I pulled myself upright and stalked back into the house. Water dripped from my hair. My nightdress clung to my body, showing bones where it had once shown curves. In a perverse way, I liked this, was so pleased I lit a lamp and went to observe myself before the looking glass in the hall.

As I swiveled from one side to the other, I realized that Rob had been right. I did look like a boy. Only the wet braid, hanging like a slimy snake down the center of my spine, spoiled the effect.

Hurrying to the kitchen, I put down the lamp and took hold of the poultry shears. The braid slid from my neck to the floor. It lay there like a dead thing. Using a towel so my hands would not have to come in contact with it, I retrieved my hair and dumped it into the slop bucket.

When I passed the mirror a second time, what I saw was altogether pleasing. I saw someone I liked. It was Nell Edmonds. She was lean and smooth. Her belly was flat. A cap of sleek hair clung to her head. But she didn't look like a boy, more like a very young girl—a strong and wiry one whose eyes glinted with a strange yellow fire and whose fingers were long and thin and ringless.

Nell stood there for a while looking at herself. Then, satisfied, she extinguished the lamp and went back up to her bed. Without changing her sopping gown, she lay flat on her back and stared at the ceiling.

Soon something wonderful happened. Nell found that she was flying effortlessly out her window and into the night sky. Like a thin white bird, she stretched her body and let herself waft on the currents of cool air. She flew higher and then higher, until she was above her farm, above Amherst, above all of Massachusetts.

Nell was elated. She was no one's prisoner anymore. She was never going to be captured again. She was light and clever. She was young and free. She liked being free.

Thursday, October 5, 1899

When Nell woke the next morning in her clammy gown and in her clammy bed, all sense of elation had vanished. Sluggishly, she rose and dressed herself. Then, not bothering to brush her matted hair, Nell went downstairs and out into the yard. It was a cold, crisp day, and when she gazed around, she could see that the trees on the hillsides and in the woods were beginning to flame with color. Could this have been going on for weeks without her noticing?

And what about Rob? Had she met him by the pump last night? Was he gone?

Rob's departure was confirmed by the damp earth beneath the pump and by one other detail—his blue cap. He'd forgotten it. He *was* gone. He had left her, and she had nothing to remember him by except his ugly, disreputable cap.

She stomped on it. She kicked it. Then she began to weep, and still weeping, she lunged again. She intended to annihilate it, but a sudden head rush speckled the world with dancing black dots. She was staggering, losing her balance, collapsing.

When Nell woke up, she was in her bed, covered with quilts, packed in with hot-water bottles. Around her stood her father, her mother, and Eliza. Dr. Sternhagen was there, too.

Mama knelt at Nell's side, reached under the covers, and took hold of her hand. "You're ill, honeypot, but we're going to see that you get better."

Tears ran from Nell's eyes and dribbled down into her ears. She thought Mama looked unwell. Her face was taut, yellowish. Nell felt sorry for her mother, but she felt sorrier for herself.

"Don't cry, Nellie. You've just had some kind of spell, but everything will be all right. We'll look after you. You don't have to do a thing—except eat and begin to regain your strength."

Nell closed her eyes and let her head roll sideways on the pillow.

"Has she fainted again?" Mama asked.

Someone else took hold of her hand, then her wrist. She knew it must be Dr. Sternhagen because he smelled of ether. "We must expect relapses," he said. "These cases are difficult."

Nell lay with her eyes shut and listened to the voices. They talked about her as if she weren't present.

"Will she recover?" Papa asked. He sounded angry. Nell wondered if he cared or if he was simply interested in trading her to Anson Tanner in return for a loan.

"Most probably," Dr. Sternhagen replied. "But melancholia can be stubborn."

Mama spoke next. "How stubborn?"

"Oh, Mrs. Edmonds, to cure this condition takes patience and understanding."

Then Dr. Sternhagen began to talk of extra doses of elixir and of food. Every time he mentioned food, Nell's stomach contracted. He was recommending lentil soup and liver and lima beans and stewed tomatoes.

At last, convinced that—even on an empty stomach—she was going to gag or retch, Nell opened her eyes.

"I'll eat," she said, "but only white foods."

"White foods?" her mother asked.

Nell nodded. "Milk, rice, potatoes, white bread . . ."

"What are you talking about?" Her mother's voice was not nearly so comforting now. It was sharper, irritable.

". . . or yellow—pale, pale yellow like chicken broth or custard," Nell whispered. "My stomach won't tolerate anything with color." Before anyone could answer, she closed her eyes again.

"We won't aggravate you unnecessarily," Dr. Sternhagen told her. "We'll ask Mother to cater to these whims. At least for a while. You'll do that, won't you, Mrs. Edmonds?"

"Of course . . ."

They'd cater to her whims? Nell might like that. It could put an end to her ordeal. She was pleased.

She began to relax. Then the doctor's fingers probed at her eyelids, pulling them up. "Anything else?" he asked, forcing her to keep looking at him. "Have you anything else to say?"

"Yes, I don't believe I shall be able to marry Anson Tanner."

After Nell had been reassured that she was too unwell to be anyone's bride, she was encouraged to stop worrying and to sleep. She pretended to acquiesce by keeping her eyes closed so she wouldn't have to converse with her family as they tiptoed in and out of her room. Later, Mama produced Dr. Sternhagen's medicine, and Nell swallowed it obediently. When her dinner appeared, she took three spoonfuls of chicken broth and two small bites of a white biscuit, before she asked to be left alone.

"I'm tired. I'll finish in a while," she said.

As soon as she was by herself, she poured the soup into the chamber pot under her bed. To dispose of the biscuits, she knelt at her window and crumbled them down into the lilac bushes below, where the birds could feast on them.

As long as she didn't let herself remember that Rob had deserted her, she was calm. But every time she thought of him, she began to weep. If she could go outdoors, she'd feel more like herself. But she couldn't do that yet. First, she had to rein herself in, learn how to be a convincing invalid. And that would not be easy.

By mid-afternoon, she was writhing with boredom. Nell the Good, Nell the Strong, was never sick, never confined to bed. It was a busy day in a busy season. She could smell the apple cider that her mother and Eliza were pressing. Farther off, behind the barn, the sound of strange men's voices told her Papa had hired dayworkers to help harvest the onions. All these activities were going on without her. How odd. How aggravating.

Late in the afternoon Eliza, looking exhausted, dragged herself into Nell's room. "You certainly chose a fine time to be sick! And what did you do to your hair?"

Nell reached a hand up and raked it through the ragged mop on her head. Until that instant, no one had mentioned her hair. She shook it so it got wilder, covering her forehead, her eyes. Then she pushed it back again.

"If you'll get me my quilt, I'll explain."

Eliza sighed at being asked to go up and down the stairs, but she did it. "All right. Now—tell me."

"I will. In a minute."

Nell spread the crazy quilt over herself, over the whole bed. She took out a saffron thread and began to embroider crow's-feet near the black velvet diamond in its center. She pulled languidly at her needle. She wasn't in a hurry anymore. Now the quilt could take forever. She wasn't going to marry Anson Tanner this month, so she could just keep on embroidering, covering every inch of the velvet with fancy stitching.

Finally Nell spoke. "I cut it with the poultry shears."

"How could you have done such a thing?"

"I'm not sure."

"But you look terrible, Nellie, absolutely dreadful. Someone's going to have to even it up, neaten it. Do something."

"Probably."

Eliza pushed aside one edge of the quilt and sat down next to Nell. "It is gorgeous, truly gorgeous," she sighed.

"My hair?"

"No, no." Eliza giggled. "Your quilt. I covet it. I wish I could do something like this. I wish I—well, look, Nellie, I don't understand anything. I thought you were making it for when you got married, that you wanted to marry Cousin Anson. What do you want? What do you really want?"

"I don't know. I'm not thinking clearly."

"Who is? Who can with so much to do? And with Rob gone, there'll be even more work."

"If you'll help me, I'll help you."

Eliza's eyes narrowed. "How?"

"Make sure Mama's put the wedding dress away. Tell her it will make me gravely ill to see it again. Let me know when Papa has spoken to Anson Tanner. And, if you do those things for me, I'll help more about the house again."

"Is that all you want?"

No, Nell wanted other things—many other things which she couldn't discuss with her sister. Eliza would never understand. Nor would Papa. Or Mama. But Nell is taking charge now. No one shall make her say yes again when she wants to say no. Nell will make rules, stricter rules than ever, and that is how she'll get herself from one day to another.

"Liza, there is one more thing."

"What?"

"Rob's cap. Would you fetch it for me?"

"Why would you want that? After you finished stomping on it, Mama threw it in the ragbag."

"Well, fish it out, please."

Rolling her eyes, Eliza nodded. "All right, but first you must answer a question for me. Where's your braid?"

Nell didn't understand why Eliza cared about her chopped-off hair. "What difference does it make?"

"Well, maybe we can save it, make a bun to pin on at the nape of your neck."

"I doubt it," Nell said.

"Why not? What did you *do* with it?"

"Put it in the slop bucket."

Eliza's eyes opened wide. "The slop bucket? The slop bucket? Why, that means—"

"—that the pigs have eaten it!"

"The pigs! The pigs have eaten your hair!"

Somehow, at that moment, it was such a wonderfully ridiculous notion that Eliza and Nell sat on the bed side by side rocking with laughter.

Thursday, October 26, 1899

These days, Nell is spending a good deal of her time either laughing or crying. Although this upsets her family, she doesn't care, because she is freer than she's ever been. The white brocade wedding dress has been packed away. No one mentions it or marriage to Anson Tanner, and no one's asked what's become of his ring.

Since Nell continues to be faithful about taking Dr. Sternhagen's elixir, she's been able to convince her mother that she doesn't have to remain in bed. Now, with freakish bursts of energy, she flies about the house, assuming her usual share of household tasks. All she needs, she tells herself as she rushes to and fro with her shorn hair prickling the nape of her neck, is a broomstick to complete the witchy way she feels.

Today, by noon, she'd already baked a cake for Eliza's eighteenth birthday, trimmed the lamps, and swept the floors. She'd also dug beets from the garden, picked some winter squash, and mixed a batch of dough for cracked-wheat bread. Cooking had begun to give her particular satisfaction. The kitchen smells were delicious, and the more she produced for the family, the less attention they seemed to pay to what she consumed.

As she waited for the dough to rise, she spread the quilt in her lap and began to embroider around the edge of the fawn and ecru dahlia in the center of Eliza's block. What she was doing had a subtlety that pleased her. She had chosen to render her sister's age in Roman numerals—XVIII, XVIII, XVIII. For almost three months, she and Eliza would be the same age.

Eighteen was so young, and Nell was so clever. She would never stop decorating this quilt. It would be her life's work, stretching on before her in an endless procession of days. Mama encouraged Nell to work on it, believing it had a calming effect on her otherwise frenetic ways.

As Nell was threading her needle, about to start another XVIII, Mama said that it was time for midday dinner.

"I'll get Papa," Nell volunteered. "Then I'm going to have a picnic in the woods."

Her mother frowned and stuffed her hands into the pockets of her apron. "But, Nellie, we'd like—"

"Not today." She'd been industrious and deserved a day off. "Before it's too late, I want to see the fall colors. And, while I'm there, maybe I'll gather chestnuts."

"But you mustn't miss dinner."

Nell slid from the kitchen stool and, struggling to control her temper, began to stuff the quilt into its too-small basket. "I *said* I'd take a picnic." As she spoke, her eyes filled with tears. She let them roll down her cheeks.

"Don't," Mama said, lifting one corner of her apron and using it to blot Nell's eyes. "It's all right, honeypot. Don't get weepy. You're doing so well. You seem heartier. So have your walk. It'll stir up an appetite for Liza's birthday supper."

A short while later, Nell was strolling toward the woods with the basket over her arm. It contained her crazy quilt and a hot baked potato wrapped in a square of flannel. She wondered how many bites she could make the potato last. She'd have to count as she ate it.

She loosened the shawl about her shoulders. Then, glancing down, she congratulated herself because Mama was convinced she was heartier. When she raised her eyes, she saw Tobias over to her left, with a wheelbarrow full of pumpkins from the Hoffmans' garden.

The look he gave her now was different—not the hungry leer she'd come to expect. Instead, Tobias appeared to be laughing at her. The corners of her mouth tightened. She'd never looked better. So what could he—oh, yes. Rob's blue hat was on her head. Well, let him laugh. It was warm, and these days Nell found it was hard to ward off the cold.

Soon she'd left Tobias behind. She was in the woods, where frost had turned the maples red, the elms golden. Their brightness assaulted her eyes. She saw color everywhere—from the low-growing leaves of the wild grape to the clusters of ripened berries hanging high over her head. She felt, all of a sudden, as if she'd never truly appreciated the fall foliage.

But it was cool beneath the trees, so she searched until she found an open patch with a leaf-strewn circle of sunshine. There, she shook out the quilt, put it on the ground.

She stretched out on it and split open her potato. She was full long before she finished its warm, dry meat. She held the rest of it between her hands until its heat had drained away. Then she tossed it aside.

"Stop sassing me, missy. We've had about enough from you. Do you know how you're tearing up our lives?"

"I'm not doing anything to you."

"Whatever you do to yourself, Nell, you do to us. So it's about time you stopped this demented behavior."

She tried to blink them back, but tears spilled from her eyes. "So I can marry Anson Tanner? So I can keep you out of debt?"

"That's a vile accusation, young lady. And stop whimpering. It may work with the others, but not with me."

"But, Papa, no one listens. I wanted college and to go to Boston."

"Dreams. Foolishness."

"I don't wish to lead Mama's life."

"Is your mother's life so bad? Have you ever asked her? Besides, your life *was* going to be different—living in town with a fine man and a fine child."

"But I didn't want it. Not any of it."

"You're unnatural," Papa said, with a scowl.

"Please go away. Please leave me alone."

"Oh, you'll be alone all right," Papa said, his voice growing louder. "Forever and ever alone and six feet deep. Is that what you want? Is it? Answer me!"

Before Nell could speak, her mother came hurrying down the hall. "Jason, no," she cried, "You mustn't. We mustn't. Don't ever. We—"

Catching hold of Papa, she pulled him out of the kitchen and closed the door behind them. Then the whispers started again. Well, Mama was whispering. Papa's voice sounded more like a low growl. Nell pushed the kitchen table up against the door so they would not disturb her. She put more coal into the stove and readjusted the kettles of water.

They were simmering, but that would not do. She was not going to have her bath until they had come to a full, rolling boil.

While she waited, listening to her parents' voices subside and their footsteps retreat upstairs, she dragged the bathing tub from the utility room to the center of the kitchen and began to fill the bucket at the tap. Over and over again, she poured water into the tub. Soon she was panting from the exertion, and she was no longer cold. Perspiration dripped from her face and made her gown cling to her body. The coals glowed through the chinks in the stove and the kitchen was wreathed in clouds of steam.

The kettles were ready. In another minute or two she'd be floating in a sea of warmth. All she had to do was draw the curtains so no one could look in. She didn't actually have to draw them, because the windows were opaque with steam, but, knowing the kitchen would cool, Nell stepped forward. As she reached out, one arm slid along the cold pane, clearing an arc of glass.

Nell was startled to see someone in the yard holding a kerosene lantern. And that person was staring in her direction. For a moment, she thought she was seeing a ghost. But no—it was someone she knew. Rob. He hadn't deserted her. He'd come back. She grabbed a dishcloth and tried to clear the window.

Because droplets of water were obscuring her view, she had to keep wiping and wiping. But she could see enough to know she'd been wrong. It wasn't Rob. It was Ludie, wrapped in Tobias's jacket. The snow was so deep it came up to her knees.

As Nell peered out, Ludie raised one hand and beckoned

Mama's mouth tightened, but she merely asked Eliza to bring her a paring knife.

Knife in hand, Eliza turned toward Nell. "Isn't the corn bread ready yet?"

"No," Nell said. "Soon . . ."

"But I need it to finish the stuffing! Then I have to get the crimping pins out of my hair, and Mama must put hers in a pompadour. If you keep being so poky, Cousin Anson will be here before we have time to change."

Nell turned her back on her sister, sighing. Yes, Anson Tanner was coming to dinner with his mother and with Jewel. Nell hadn't seen him in more than a month. When he came, though, she knew he'd be very gallant, perceiving immediately that she was now too young and too frail to leave home.

He'd understand better than her own father, she decided, as Papa—laden with wood—opened the door and stomped into the kitchen. "It's not half bad out there," he said, kicking the door closed with his boot. "Slippery from thawing and freezing. But at least it's fair." Papa addressed his words to Mama and Eliza. His eyes avoided Nell as if she weren't there.

Anson Tanner wouldn't behave that way. He was a sensitive man, with whom Nell had no quarrel. She'd even agreed, in order to be presentable for him and for his mother, to let Mama pin up her shorn hair and try to conceal its unsightliness under a black silk bow.

As she finished pouring the pumpkin purée into its crust, she turned toward Mama and Eliza. They were discussing Ludie.

"What about her?" Nell asked.

Mama turned toward Nell. "Does that filling have enough cinnamon? Enough nutmeg?"

"I'm not sure."

"Didn't you taste it?"

"No, it's too dark."

Mama winced. "Oh, Nell."

"Here, you can have a taste. Take a lick from the spoon."

"No. No. I'm sure it will be fine."

Eliza ignored the interchange about the spices for the pumpkin pie, and kept talking as if she and Mama had never been interrupted. "Oh, Ludie must be *so* happy!"

"What about Ludie?" Nell demanded, clamoring to be heard.

Mama continued to chop the giblets. "She's expecting again. Claire Hoffman told me yesterday."

Eliza cradled a dish towel in her arms. "A new baby to start out the twentieth century. How thrillingly appropriate. It's coming, you know, the new century."

Nell didn't feel any joyous anticipation. She wasn't sure Ludie did, either. Nor did Mama seem enthusiastic.

"Nellie, you'd better check that corn bread."

"Mmm . . ." Nell agreed, reaching for a broomstraw, opening the oven door. When the straw came out clean, she took a towel and lifted the pan from the oven. Then she slid her pies in its place.

Eliza rattled on. "A new century. New life. And Papa says the mare is in foal and that the tabby got out when she was in season."

Mama frowned. "If there are kittens, he's going to drown them. He says we must stop contributing to the feral cat population of Amherst."

Nell shuddered. But no one noticed. She was becoming

so small she was nearly invisible. Sometimes no one saw her at all. Clasping her arms across her chest, she fled from the room. Papa, kneeling before the fireplace, didn't turn as she flew past.

Nell was dressed in the blue serge with a darkish pinafore over it and many layers of undergarments beneath. Mama had done the best she could with Nell's hair—slicking, pinning, trying to hide it under the bow. Nell didn't mind the bow. It was childish but becoming. She'd even gone to stand before the looking glass to admire her sculptured cheeks and angular jawline.

She had to share the glass with her sister, of course. Eliza, dressed in Nell's rose-colored merino, looked charming, though a bit too round. And she'd done her hair in a new way, put up in back with a cluster of curls cascading over each ear.

"Pinch your cheeks, Nellie," she suggested. "That's what I did."

"I look fine," Nell said. "Just fine."

"Girls! Hurry," Mama called, putting an end to their exchange. "The gravy isn't finished and we haven't braised the carrots."

A few moments later, Nell, trembling with cold despite her winter cloak, was out in the root cellar. Trying to move as quickly as she could without growing dizzy, she pawed through a basket of sawdust to fetch the carrots they had forgotten earlier in the day. When the door creaked open, she stiffened, half expecting to find Tobias poking his nose in where he had no business to be. She was wrong. It was Anson Tanner.

Nell's apron was covered with sawdust, and hanks of

loosening hair were escaping from behind her ears. Embarrassed, she scrambled to her feet. She had to clutch at the stone wall to steady herself and pretend she wasn't blacking out. Just as she thought she was going to, cold air from the open door restored her equilibrium.

"Good afternoon," Anson Tanner said, averting his eyes from Nell's face. Once she would have assumed he was being tactful about the broken-off engagement, but he was acting exactly like Papa. She was an inconvenience, and he didn't care for the way she looked.

Well, it was Anson Tanner's loss. She didn't intend to marry him in the spring any more than she had intended to wed him in October.

He volunteered to carry the carrots for her.

"Thank you. But I can manage them. And a good deal more if I care to."

Then, as if she were unaware that he'd crooked his arm to help her across the icy yard, she made her way back to the house.

Once dinner was ready, Nell insisted on serving it. That way she rid herself of the necessity of sitting too long at the table, of eating too much, or of holding polite conversations with any of them. Mrs. Tanner, like her son, tried to avoid looking at Nell. But Jewel stared and stared.

The sole thing that kept the meal from being a disaster was that Eliza chattered like a magpie, making everyone smile—even Anson Tanner and his stern mother.

Later, after the last slice of pie had been consumed, they left the table and moved to the parlor for coffee. Nell tried to avoid accompanying them by staying behind to do the dishes, but Mama, with great firmness, said no.

So, while Nell and the others balanced their coffee cups,

Jewel sat in a child-sized rocking chair Papa had made for Eliza when she was young. Jewel's scrawny hands were clasped in her lap.

"Sit up," Mrs. Tanner told her. "Shoulders back. Don't slump. Your mother was stooped, and straws show which way the wind blows."

Jewel straightened her shoulders. "Granny?" she asked, softly. Nell leaned forward. She wanted to hear what the child had to say.

"Not now," Mrs. Tanner told her. "Later. And put your knees together. A young lady crosses her feet at the ankles."

Nell was so tired it was difficult to restrain herself. She wanted to start giggling uncontrollably or crying. That child, Anson Tanner's Jewel, couldn't be more than five and she was expected to behave like an adult. Only five and her life was already dreadful.

"Jewel, don't stare. It's not polite."

Nell glowered at Mrs. Tanner. Then she glanced around the room. There wasn't one female in the room, not one, whose life she'd like to live—including her own. Except, perhaps, Eliza, who always remembered that being selfish helped.

Nell's hair kept springing out from under its bow, but she'd given up on it. She struggled to keep the room in a clear focus. Wheels of darkness spun before her eyes. She pinched herself, and found that it helped, so she did it again, harder.

Anson Tanner was examining his shoes and, it appeared, everyone else's, too. Well, after all, that was his business. Perhaps shoes were of greater interest to him than the way his mother was treating his daughter.

"Granny?" Jewel said again.

"Shush, dear. This is a grownup evening, and you are fortunate to be included."

Unexpectedly, Eliza clanked her cup into its saucer and rose to her feet. "She's just a little girl, Mrs. Tanner, and I think you're being too hard on her."

Nell, stunned by her sister's audacity, expected that Eliza would be reprimanded by her parents or by Mrs. Tanner. But it didn't happen. Anson Tanner looked up approvingly, and Mrs. Tanner sent a smile in Eliza's direction.

Jewel, emboldened by this tacit acceptance of her right to be a child, suddenly spoke. But instead of speaking to her grandmother, she addressed her question directly to Nell. "How come," she asked, "you look so much like Marco's monkey?"

❦

Monday, December 25, 1899

It's Christmas. Joy to the World. Or is that merely an ironic hope with no possibility of fulfillment? Nell has no answer to this question. In fact, as a person who had come to look like Marco's monkey, she has no answers to anything.

Her memory—because of Dr. Sternhagen's tonic, perhaps—is not as keen as it used to be, and the weeks since Thanksgiving have passed in a blur. Only by disciplining herself rigorously has she managed to hem and initial squares of linen as gifts for her family. But she begrudged every moment they took, for they stole time she needed to decorate and redecorate the hundreds of patches in her quilt.

Now, with her gifts finished and presented, she could take it up again. She was pleased to feel it on her lap, pleased that her family had gone without her to church and then to pay a holiday call on the Tanners.

"I'm sorry to leave you," Mama had said as she kissed her goodbye. "But it *is* best you stay in, Nellie. It's snowy, and I don't want you to catch a chill."

"If they have sugar plums at the Tanners'," Eliza told her, twirling to make her new green cape undulate about her body, "I'll bring you a white one."

Papa's brow was furrowed. He said goodbye, but when he leaned down to kiss her, his lips didn't touch her cheek. Maybe he thinks her condition is catching. Maybe it is.

Nell was glad to have the house to herself, to be there alone with the tabby. After Thanksgiving, Nell had moved the cat from the barn to her room. Now she feeds her food from her own plate. Under the bed, next to the chamber pot, Nell keeps a bowl of water and a box of clean wood chips, which the tabby uses for elimination purposes.

Nell doesn't know when the kittens will be born, but each day she can see the cat's belly stretching lower toward the ground. The tabby's not a particularly demonstrative creature, but she seems lazily contented in her new quarters. The animal, always seeking warmth, spends the long nights curled next to Nell. While she sits there wide awake, the cat—like a living hot-water bag—helps to ward off the cold.

Sometimes she's a nuisance, pulling at Nell's embroidery threads or pouncing at the quilt as it moves on her knees. Other times, Nell puts down her needle and examines the animal. When Nell blows at the fur, she sees a multicolored iridescence, with each hair black, white, gray, and a glowing ginger all at the same time. She also sees the delicate pink of skin at its roots. A pink-gold that pulses with life.

Nell's skin, if it was ever like that, is not that way anymore. What Jewel said on Thanksgiving may have been rude—out of the mouths of babes, the Psalms say—but what the child voiced was true. Nell *does* look like a monkey. It just took one glance to confirm the resemblance. Now when Nell tries to avoid the glass, it pulls at her, commanding her to stare into it.

A month ago, she was pleased with her appearance, but since then her skin has become mottled and her eyes look too deeply embedded. Their odd glittering gaze sends goose tracks up and down her spine. Nell's reflection puzzles her. Sometimes she thinks it's a mirage, and if she could sneak up on herself unawares, she'd find the beautiful, strong, lean Nell she'd admired so much.

"Maybe I need some fresh air," she told the tabby. "Perhaps I'll take a walk—let the wind blow roses into my cheeks."

Nell pushed the cat and the quilt aside. Getting up, she dressed, donned a cloak, the navy-striped scarf Mama had knitted her for Christmas. Then, clapping Rob's hat on her head, she went out.

The sun upon the snow was so bright it made the hills seem strewn with diamonds. Bare tree branches thrust themselves upward and outward, looking so dark and dead that Nell was sure no leaves would ever grace them again. Only the evergreens shone with a glossy assurance that promised spring.

"Strange, unreal."

She didn't know where to go or what to do, but having made the effort to dress herself and come outside, she was not willing to give up.

"I've been lazy," she said, as ice crystals stabbed at the back of her throat, forming whirlpools that spiraled down into her belly. "I must be stricter. I must expect more."

She began to pick her way through the woods toward the pond. Not everyone was in church, celebrating the birth of Jesus, she realized, as she reached the downhill path that would bring her to its frozen edge. Skaters were racing across the ice, tiptoeing on it, falling clumsily. They were also shouting and laughing. From where Nell stood, their colorful winter garments whirled and shifted on the ice like chips of glass in a kaleidoscope.

"Why did I never notice that before?"

Because she and Rob had never stopped on the hill to watch. They'd always been part of that swirl of activity. Other winters, she and Rob had played tag, stick hockey, practiced crossovers. They chased Eliza or hid from her. They joined in at a tug-of-war or warmed their hands together over the bonfire at the south end of the pond. But Rob had deserted her. And he wasn't coming back.

To get out of the cutting wind and closer to the bonfire, she started downhill again. "Damn him. Boys can . . . men can . . ."

But her words hung unfinished in the air, as her feet skidded on a patch of ice. Tired, weak, unprepared for such a fall, Nell gave in to it and tumbled submissively down, down, and down until a tree stump brought her to a halt.

At first, she just lay there. Every hidden stone had battered her thin body. The force with which she'd hit the stump had knocked the wind out of her. Finally, she moved. But she was frightened, unsure if she was strong enough to climb back uphill toward her house. On the snowy ground, it was cold—so cold. Nothing was stirring in her immediate vicinity except birds. From afar, she heard the voices of the skaters, but close-up she heard nothing except birds twittering and flapping their wings.

"Maybe I won't get up. Perhaps, I'll lie here and go to sleep."

"No," a voice told her. "You get up."

Nell turned her head.

"You get up," the voice repeated.

Nell raised her eyes. Ludie was standing over her, pressing Rob's cap back onto her head. Nell stared up at the pregnant girl. She let Ludie pull her to her feet. She felt weak. She couldn't talk.

Walking wasn't easy either, but with Ludie to lean on, Nell began to make her way home. Despite her discomfort, she was alert enough to be ashamed that a person *she* hoped to help was helping her. What did Ludie think of her? And what had she been doing on the hillside above the pond?

When Nell had to rest, Ludie propped her against the trunk of a hickory tree and pulled crusts of dried bread from her pockets. Then Nell discovered why the girl was outside. She'd come to feed the birds. As Ludie crumbled her crusts, flocks of them gathered, fluttering and chirping at her feet.

While Nell watched, chickadees and nuthatches and finches surrounded them. A blood-red cardinal appeared. Gently, carefully, Ludie pinched at the bread and sprinkled bits of it on the ground. Only when the last crust had been strewn did Ludie turn and offer her arm to Nell again.

For a few moments, the birds chattered and followed after them. Then, one by one, they wheeled off over the white snow and against the steely-blue sky.

Nell was stiffer and colder than she had been before they'd stopped. It was all she could manage to put one foot in front of the other and keep her jaw clamped together so her teeth wouldn't clatter. Ludie assisted her. She was kind to Nell, yet she was undemonstrative.

As soon as they reached the Edmondses' yard, Ludie released her. She waited a moment to see if Nell could proceed unaided. Then she turned back toward the Hoffmans' and the cabin she shared with Tobias.

"Wait," Nell called, aware that her voice was hardly more than a croak.

Ludie paused, but her pursed lips made it plain that she felt she had done her duty. She hadn't aided Nell out of friendship or a sense of concern. She'd only been the Hoffmans' hired man's wife helping the neighbor's sickly daughter. That was the beginning and end of it.

Ludie didn't want Nell's help or friendship any more than anyone else did. Supporting Nell's bony body, looking into her monkey face seemed to have spooked her. Now she wanted to escape.

Nell wanted to escape, too, but no matter how hard she tried, it didn't seem possible. She let herself in the kitchen door. Once inside, waiting for her family, she huddled by the stove, drinking ginger tea. She wouldn't tell them she'd been out or that she'd fallen. Maybe if she moved carefully and their eyes kept passing over her head, they wouldn't notice that her body was paining her. And since she never let anyone see her without clothes anymore, they'd never know how bruised it was.

When Nell heard sleigh bells and the clop-clop of the horses in the yard, she heard her family's cheerful voices, too. But as they entered the house, they became unnaturally subdued. "I'm the cause of this," Nell reminded herself. "And I must try to make amends."

As Mama and Papa and Eliza sat down to Christmas dinner, Nell eased herself into her own straight-backed chair. Although she wanted to be upstairs in bed with the tabby pressed against her chest and a needle in her hand, she forced herself to join the others at the table. To please them, she was even going to eat a small piece of ham—if she could find a sliver from close to the bone with no slimy fat on it.

She could endure this meal without incident. Still, to give herself extra strength, she gripped the seat of her chair as Papa rose to offer his traditional holiday grace.

"Oh, Lord, we thank you for your goodness and for the blessings we are about to receive. Look upon us with kindness, but offer aid and succor also to the poor and less fortunate—those who suffer—"

Suddenly Papa's voice cracked. He stopped. He repeated himself. "And to the less fortunate—those who—"

Nell was afraid to look up, for she knew she'd see something she had never seen before—tears in Papa's eyes. He was choked up and unable to continue.

"Amen," Mama said.

Nell raised her head. Eliza was staring at her plate. Papa, swaying on his feet, was struggling to salvage himself and the rest of them, too.

"Amen," Mama repeated, somewhat more forcefully.

Papa dropped heavily into his chair. Nell closed her eyes and sat there, hardly willing to draw a breath.

Monday, January 1, 1900

Last night, everyone rang in the New Year and celebrated the beginning of a new century. The Tanners came to the Edmondses' and so did the Hoffmans. All of them were impressed to be witnessing "the turn." Over fruitcake and punch, they spoke effusively of the future.

Nell couldn't capture a shred of their excitement or a whit of curiosity about what kind of world lay ahead. The present one was so difficult that she quailed at the notion of looking ahead. But no one asked her what she thought. Especially the Hoffmans. Rob's parents were distant, as if they blamed her for the fact that he had run off. Well, Nell was frosty toward them, too. She moved through the evening like a wraith, silent and unobserved.

Only Jewel noticed her. The child must have been instructed not to mention Nell's monkey face or any other aspect of her appearance, but she did stare. Then, finally, she sidled up and asked about the crazy quilt. Grateful, Nell decided to reward her.

"Come, I'll show you. But let's go upstairs where we won't disturb the others."

Because Nell's room received heat from the floor grate vented to the parlor stove, it was reasonably warm. Nell lit a lamp. She spread the quilt on her bed, and as the two of them knelt on the floor next to it, she began to explain about Grandmother Shaw's silks and velvets.

"I don't believe it," Jewel declared. "I've been to Boston, but I never saw anyone with that many frocks."

"Your father said nearly the same thing. Some fabrics are ours and a few were probably my aunts' dresses, but they're mostly from my grandmother."

Jewel stuck a finger in her ear and wiggled it around. "Granny Tanner says it's not good to lie."

"Oh, I'm not lying."

Jewel did not seem convinced. She removed the finger from her ear and used it to trace the outlines of a patch of red-and-black-checked taffeta. "Have you ever counted them?"

"Not really," Nell answered, regretting her impulse to be nice to the child.

"Can we do it? Now."

"If you want."

"Separately or together?"

All of a sudden, Nell was tired. She wanted to lie down and rest. She wanted Jewel to disappear. "You choose."

"Why is the center so black and so ugly?" Jewel asked.

"Because I don't know what I want to put there."

"Hadn't you better decide soon?" Jewel said.

"Why?"

"Before you die," Jewel said.

"What?"

"Before you die. You are going to die, aren't you?"

Nell rocked back on her heels. Die? Who thought Nell was going to die? Her family? The Tanners? Everyone? Well, they were wrong. She wasn't. Not as long as she could keep working on her quilt, but that was too complicated to explain to Jewel.

"Would you like to see my tabby?" Nell asked.

Jewel rubbed at her eyes. "I don't like cats. They scratch."

"Mine doesn't." Nell reached out and plucked the tabby from the pillow where she'd been sleeping. Then she sat on the bed and coaxed Jewel to sit there, too. "Here, pet her."

"Granny Tanner hates cats."

"Well, Granny Tanner is downstairs, and we're up here. So go on, pet her."

Jewel's head bobbed back against the bed pillows.

"She's fat."

"That's because she's going to have babies—little baby kittens. Feel."

When Jewel asked how the kittens got inside the tabby and how they were going to get out, Nell told her.

"It sounds messy," the child said. She yawned. "I don't think I want to have babies. Do you?"

"No."

"And I'm glad you're not going to marry Pappy."

"Why?"

"Because I don't believe you like me very much, and I don't think"—as Jewel spoke, she was struggling to keep her eyes open—"that I like you either."

Nell, touched by Jewel's honesty, lifted the child and hugged her.

"You're so bony. A bag o' bones," Jewel murmured. "Granny Tanner says . . . she says . . ."

But Jewel's eyes were closing. Nell watched her for a

few moments, considered staying there and trying to steal some of Jewel's warmth and peacefulness.

She didn't, however. She was agitated. She couldn't sit still, even to sew. Sighing, she rose and covered Jewel with the crazy quilt. She arranged Jewel's head on the pillow, smoothing the carroty curls away from her face. The tabby insinuated herself closer to Jewel.

"Fickle thing. But that's all right. Maybe, if we can save your kits from Papa, we might give her one."

Then Nell slipped out of the room and began to make her way downstairs. She didn't know what time it was, but she knew it was not midnight. It couldn't be 1900 yet, because no one had shaken the clackers or rung the bells.

As she was on the stairway, she heard voices from below. They were discussing her.

"Nothing except *white* foods?"

"Have you tried Greene's Nervura or Ayer's Sarsaparilla?"

"Zack Sternhagen makes his own tonic."

"But she's so frail. Just skin and bones."

"And her coloring's chlorotic."

"We know."

"Try someone else."

"Ask for a consultation."

"Well, perhaps. Maybe."

"If she doesn't pick up soon . . ."

Nell didn't hear Eliza's voice or Anson Tanner's, but the others were enough. She wasn't going in there. Nor did she intend to linger in the hall eavesdropping. No wonder Jewel thought Nell was going to die.

"It would serve them right. They'd be sorry then."

"Nell?" someone said.

It was Mama. She was standing in the hallway with the half-finished basket in her hands. Her face was strained. She looked as if she'd been crying. "Where have you been, Nellie?"

"Putting Jewel to bed."

"Come in where it's warm, honeypot. And—here—look at your quilt basket. It's taking shape, isn't it? By your birthday, it should be done. But now, won't you have some punch with us?"

The punch was a dark grapy color. It had alcohol in it and smelled nearly as bad as Dr. Sternhagen's tonic.

"I will. Soon."

Mama put an arm around her shoulders. "What's wrong?"

Nell pulled away. "Do you like this?"

Mama looked perplexed. "Like what?"

"This. All of this. Your life? You said once you didn't want *me* to lead *your* life. Papa said I didn't understand what you'd said, that I should ask you how you felt about it. You work so hard. Do so much. Why? It's dreadful, isn't it? It's not worth it. Why do you put up with it? Why do you go on?"

"Nell . . . Nellie, calm yourself. We can't settle this now. Let's talk another time. When it's just the two of us. When we don't have company."

"Of course. I'm embarrassing enough. I shouldn't make it worse, especially not in front of your friends."

Nell moved toward the kitchen.

"Where are you going?"

She was going outside. But if she told Mama, Mama would restrain her, make her join them for the New Year's celebration. So Nell gave the one answer that ensured she would be left in peace.

"I'm hungry. I'd like to have some bread and butter."

It was an eerie night. If there was a moon, it was hidden behind clouds. Nell had stopped to slice some bread, and as she made her way across the yard, she took small bites from it. It tasted good. If she got too full, she'd crumble the rest and, like Ludie, feed it to the birds.

What about Ludie? How were she and Tobias celebrating the beginning of a new century? Nell moved past the edge of the barn so that she could see their cabin. It was dark. There was no sign of a candle or a lamp. Perhaps they'd gone to town. Yet that seemed unlikely. Perhaps they were already in bed.

Nell shivered. For a moment, she stood in the lee of the barn, thinking she'd return to the house. She'd slip past the others and go wake Jewel so the two of them could kneel at her bedroom window to observe "the turn." But Jewel would complain about being shaken from her sleep. Jewel didn't like Nell, and she'd been honest enough to say so. Why would she want to share January 1, 1900, with a monkey like Nell? Still . . .

Nell heard a familiar laugh and caught a glimpse of a green cloak. She wasn't the only one observing the last of the century. Eliza was outside, too, and she was not alone. Anson Tanner, his hands clasped behind his back, was at her side.

Nell turned and fled into the barn. She edged into the cow's stall, crouched close to the animal's warm flank. After a while, too weak and shaky to stay in that position, she crept from the stall and made her way up the ladder to the loft. Then she began to bury herself beneath the sweet-smelling hay.

By the time the church bells rang and the town cannons boomed, only Nell's head—with Rob's cap upon it—stuck out above this prickly bed. From where she lay, she could hear the bells and cannon bursts mingling with the closer sounds of excited voices shouting.

Nell was alone where no one could love her, touch her, nag her, question her, ask for her hand in marriage, urge her to eat, tell her that Boston was a pipe dream, demand false joy, or reject her all-too-real suffering.

"And they'll never find me here. Because now I'm so small, so thin, so hard to see that I am like a needle in a haystack."

Saturday, January 13, 1900

Days are like fragments now, as crazily and haphazardly patterned as the bits and pieces of Nell's quilt. Even to-day, her birthday, was a series of disconnected, overlapping moments, which began, not long after first light, when Nell was sitting in bed stitching and Mama knocked at the door.

"Come in," Nell told her.

In recent days, Nell had stopped embroidering decorative borders, because almost every patch on her quilt had one. Instead, she'd gone back to the unadorned squares of silk or velvet. To the quilt that was strewn with flowers and beautiful things, Nell had begun adding other kinds of images—spiders, beetles, roaches, maggots, and any manner of slimy, crawling creatures.

No one in her family had commented on Nell's newest designs, yet the discomfort they experienced when examining them was obvious. This morning when Mama approached the bed, coming close enough to see the nearly completed blue newt, she shuddered.

Then, composing herself, she leaned forward and gave Nell a kiss on her cheek. "Happy birthday," she said. "See—it's done."

Mama had the black ash basket in her arms. It was finished. Nell fixed her needle in a patch of wren-brown moiré. She reached out. "Thank you, I know you labored over this."

"But it was a labor of *love*," Mama said. "Because it was for you. Because I knew you needed it for your quilt."

Nell looked down, past the basket, at the quilt spread over her limbs. The tabby was sleeping on the other end, atop Grandmother Shaw's white rose. Yes, the basket had been something she needed. It was bigger and finer than the one she'd been using. But now the quilt had grown so large and so heavy it might not fit in this new basket.

Besides, the quilt would not need a container much longer. Once it was finished, it would be spread out, displayed, cherished. Never again would it be confined.

"Here," Mama said, tugging at one corner of the quilt. "Let's put it in the basket. Then you can bring it down to breakfast. It's your birthday, and we want to spend it with you. That's why we did the washing on Sunday."

Nell pulled away. "No. Don't. Not yet. Not now."

Aware of the crestfallen look on her mother's face, Nell relented. "Oh, Mama, thank you. The basket is splendid.

I'm very pleased. But give me a few minutes. I'll join you soon."

Despite her words, Nell dawdled as she rose and dressed herself. By the time she made her way down to the kitchen, an hour had passed. Eliza had wandered off, and her parents had begun their morning work. Mama was sprinkling and rolling clothes, while Papa fetched coal to keep the stove hot enough for the irons.

"Happy birthday," Papa told Nell as he stepped back inside. Putting down the scuttle, he came to hug her. Nell felt him shudder as his arms encircled her bony shoulders.

Nell should have volunteered to help Mama with the ironing. But Nell seldom helped with anything anymore. She didn't have enough energy left from her work on the quilt. She didn't know if Eliza was taking up the slack or not. Mama looked worse and worse. Was it too much worry or too much work? Nell couldn't concentrate on finding answers to these questions. Besides, the Connecticut Valley was experiencing a January thaw, and she wanted to be outside.

"What will you do this morning?" Mama asked, as she spat on an iron to test how hot it was.

Summoning her strength, Nell said she wanted to take a walk. Mama's face brightened, as if she thought that Nell's health was taking a turn for the better. Nell hadn't taken a walk in weeks. Not since the day she'd slipped and been rescued by Ludie.

Mama's enthusiasm made Nell want to go back upstairs to sew. Instead, she accepted the woolen shawl Mama insisted she wear. Then, without offering any departing words, she wandered off.

Ludie was near her cabin, pinning up her wash. Nell

squinted, trying to decide if Ludie's baby had begun to show, but the girl's oversize dress hung loosely over her shapeless body. Nell was sure Ludie knew she was there, yet no amount of staring made Ludie look over and acknowledge her presence.

Shrugging, Nell turned away. She headed toward the woods. Tobias was in the sugar bush, pulling plugs from the trees to monitor the sap. Nell skirted around him, but she needn't have bothered. He didn't even raise his head as she passed.

Instead of walking down toward the pond, Nell crossed through the bare woods toward a little hilltop graveyard she and Rob used to visit from time to time. It was a neglected place, with the names half eroded away by the harshness of a hundred New England winters. The names on the stones were the same—Alden, Alden, Alden. It had been a plot belonging to a family that had long since died off.

Once, she and Rob had spent a whole summer day in this spot. Lying on their backs, their heads resting against separate stones, they'd talked about his plans and hers. At the time, it had been a lovely thing to do. But now Nell shuddered at the idea of stretching out above someone's body. There was nothing below except bones. Just bones. Well, she was aboveground and was hardly more than bones. She turned and fled.

After a moment, exhausted, she had to slow to a snail's pace. From up where she was, she could see for miles. On the far horizon, the shadows of the Holyoke Mountains were visible. She could see the town, the fields, a mill or two, the river, the pond. The countryside was still an unpromising winter brown; yet, under the bright sun, it glowed with uncanny clarity.

"Why did it never look this way when I was strong?"

Perhaps it was a mirage produced by her condition or by Dr. Sternhagen's vile tonic. Standing with her shawl hanging loosely from her shoulders, she admired the nearby wonders, also—a darting hare, buds on the quince bushes, a flock of mourning doves.

She considered making her way to the pond. It was, because of the unseasonal weather, half thawed. Nell saw places where water was pooling up over the ice. Once there, she could walk across the ice, straight out, until it cracked and admitted her.

Without Rob's assistance, she would not be strong enough to pull herself out or to climb back up the hill. She imagined herself lying on the pond bottom in the muck with a shelf of thawing ice above her. She shuddered.

As she turned away, she seemed to hear someone calling. "Nell . . . Nell, I dare you."

It was a strange voice. Disembodied. Nell was alone, yet someone who sounded like Rob was talking to her—Rob, whom she hadn't heard from since he'd left three months ago. She bit her bottom lip. Well, she'd walked on the ice when he dared her. And she'd taken his last dare, too. The one about Anson Tanner. Even if he'd never know it.

"I did it. I am *not* going to marry Anson Tanner."

The voice was persistent. "I dare you," it repeated. "Dare you, dare you."

"Why? What?"

She couldn't silence the voice. She had neither the

strength nor the concentration to figure it out. But it grew faint as she turned and headed toward home. Pleasurable images began to claim her attention. Visions of Grandmother Shaw going from place to place in Boston in her many elegant dresses, working for women's rights, women's suffrage. Her grandmother's frocks—the burgundy striped damask, the peach cretonne, the red-and-black taffeta, the midnight-blue velvet, the Nile-green satin, the ecru brocade, the brown foulard . . .

Because it was Nell's birthday, Eliza came home for midday dinner. Mama had managed, along with the ironing, to prepare a special meal for Nell. Foods Nell liked and could stomach—chicken and mashed potatoes and biscuits. And for dessert, a pale yellow pound cake.

Nell did take several bites. She bestirred herself enough to contribute a comment or two about her morning's walk, but to have so much food on her plate was upsetting. And because of the energy expended during the morning, she was so fatigued she could hardly chew or swallow.

"I'm tired. I must rest."

Her family exchanged distraught looks, but they made no attempt to stop her. So Nell, concealing a napkin filled with chicken breast for the tabby, slipped away from the table and went upstairs. Her room was chilly, and Mama's black ash basket sat on her bed, reminding her what an ungrateful person she was.

As she stood there, her teeth began to chatter. It had been warmer outside. Moving toward the window, she pushed it open and leaned out. Below, she saw Eliza sweeping the front steps. Nell stared at her sister, but Eliza didn't look up.

Soon she heard Mama and Papa talking. Their words drifted up to where she sat on the edge of her bed.

"Are you sure about Anson?"

"Yes. He says he'd be very happy."

"But isn't it too soon, Jason?"

"Perhaps not. Not if she's ready. And by then she might be."

"We haven't discussed it with her."

"But it's not so farfetched. Nineteen is a reasonable age."

Nell didn't feel nineteen was a reasonable age. She was no different today than she'd been yesterday when she was eighteen. What did a birthday mean, after all? A child's rhyme about the days of the week ran through her head. On what day of the week had she been born? She must be a Wednesday's child—for "Wednesday's child is full of woe." She wanted to ask Mama, but she was too weary. She didn't have enough strength to kneel at the window and call out her question.

At last, with a shrug, she picked up her old basket and prepared to transfer its contents to the new one Mama had made. The fingers that reached down and scooped out the threads and unused scraps of fabric looked like bird claws.

Farther down in the basket, she found paper patterns, transfers she'd never used, a few stray ribbons. Something was wedged in down at the bottom, a packet Nell hadn't bothered to open or examine. She loosened it from its hiding place. Nell was tempted to throw it away without looking at it. But a voice whispered, "I dare you . . ."

Holding her breath, Nell unfolded the paper. She spread it out upon her crazy quilt, flattened it so she could see what was printed on it.

Jordan Marsh.

She exhaled. That was just the name of a store in Boston. Why had she been alarmed? Now she could crumple it up and dispose of it. Just then she noticed something else. Over in one corner, beyond the words "Jordan Marsh": "Three hundred samples. No two alike."

Stunned, Nell dropped back on her pillows. So Anson Tanner and his Jewel had been right. These weren't fabrics from her grandmother's garments. They were nothing but remnants ordered from a dry-goods store. Like the transfer and the thread packets, they were part of a kit! A terrible, loathsome, unoriginal, commercial, impersonal kit. Nell hadn't been stitching her heritage together. She'd been wasting her life on something Grandmother Shaw had purchased but never touched, because it was too insignificant to take up *her* time.

Friday, February 2, 1900

The crazy quilt is a dead thing. Over. Gone. Nell doesn't care for it anymore. The blue newt remains unfinished, its needle embedded in brown moiré. Although the quilt, with its Jordan Marsh store-bought fabrics, is still spread across her bed, she feels no pride, takes no care of it. Instead, she lies on it, doesn't mind if water spills or the tabby sharpens her claws there.

These days, Nell hardly stirs from her room. She remains in bed, counting the boards in the ceiling above her head. But she keeps losing count. People sit with her— sometimes Mama or Papa. Nell knows that Papa doesn't like to see the tabby in her room, but he seems afraid to say so, unwilling to deprive her of any bit of comfort she can have.

Some evenings, Eliza glides in and stays to keep her company. If Nell were stronger, she'd ask about the dishcloths and hand towels that her sister is hemming and decorating. Never has Eliza, unless coerced, taken a needle into her hand. So why is she sewing now? But the answer, if Nell possessed it, probably wouldn't matter much to her one way or another.

As Nell's body has shrunken, so has her world. She's slight enough now to slip through a keyhole or down a drain, so small that she can be sustained on liquids—broth, finely chopped chowder, warm milk, or cider. She does, however, take them regularly. She's too tired to be anything except passive and obedient. The only thing she refuses to swallow is Dr. Sternhagen's tonic, which makes her retch with such violence that Mama has put it away.

Nell doesn't need to go out to the privy anymore. As her body has ceased to produce monthly blood, it has also stopped making solid waste. But she doesn't mind. Moving from her bed to the chamber pot is, in and of itself, a monumental effort. Her body is stranger and stranger. Sometimes in the middle of the night when she is alone, she disrobes—despite the cold—and examines herself.

Her breasts are almost nonexistent. Her abdomen's concave. Her hipbones stretch the skin and protrude sharply both front and back. Her legs and arms resemble bean poles, with strange, ugly, oversize knobs at the joints. But the strangest thing, the most secret and frightening thing about her body, is its hair.

Her back, her arms, even her belly have sprouted a covering of it. Not taffy brown like the hair on her head, but dark as fur. Monkey fur, perhaps. Or dusky like the down of young fledglings. Sometimes she imagines she might be turning into a monkey or a bird, except that she hasn't the strength to swing or fly from tree to tree.

Today when Dr. Sternhagen came, he'd insisted on examining Nell beneath her gown and undervests. But she hadn't wanted him to know about her secret fur.

"No, you can't. It's my body. You must not. No one shall . . ."

She'd blacked out then. By the time she came to, she was tucked under the covers, and she was alone. She could hear Papa, Mama, and Dr. Sternhagen whispering outside her room. Whispers, more whispers. Had they examined her, found her secret fur? If so, that's not what was being discussed.

"Has she had prior seizures?"

"Not like this."

"Well, this won't be the last. Unless we can persuade her to take more nourishment."

"We try! We try and try and keep on trying!"

"I know. But it isn't working, is it? Perhaps you should take her to Brattleboro or Stafford Springs for the waters."

"No, that's not possible. Not now. She's not strong enough."

"Not nearly."

"Then we'll simply have to wait. And hope."

"Wait and hope? That's all?"

"Yes, that's all. Now it's a question of time."

Unable to listen any longer, Nell closed her eyes, and let herself drift into a restless, twilight sleep. Flying and creeping creatures surrounded her. Hot beef briskets, edged by mottled skirts of fat, and loaves of crusty, fresh-baked bread floated into view. Yet, no matter how slyly she moved, the bread and brisket remained elusive, out of reach.

And though she yearned to lift into the air as the birds did, she was earthbound. The birds flew from her as inexorably as the beetles and roaches moved toward her. She was in some cage or prison, a place she herself had fashioned. Sometimes it seemed safe, but at others it was horrific, dangerous, and she longed for escape.

Midday, Mama returned with an eggnog and creamed-chicken broth. Mama looked so harassed and so ill that Nell struggled and managed to finish it.

"Eliza's home," Mama offered, by way of conversation. "She left school at midday to help with the sugaring. We're working indoors in the sugarhouse. Because it's *so* much earlier and so much colder than last year. Remember last year?"

Nell nodded. Yes, she did. She'd burned her hand.

In the afternoon, as Nell was dozing, the tabby at last gave birth to her kittens. Not on the nest of straw and rags that Papa had prepared in the bottom of her closet, but on the crazy quilt. When Nell opened her eyes, she could see the tiny kits, their eyes sealed shut, and the tabby consuming the bloody, gelatinous afterbirth. Blood and other slime was smeared across Rob's block, Jewel's, and on the strange black square in the center.

There'd be stains, of course. But Nell didn't care, because the quilt didn't mean anything to her anymore. Still, she took the effort to raise herself from the bed. Ignoring the tabby's hissing, she moved the four throbbing kits to the closet. Then, using a towel and her basin, she attempted to wipe up the mess.

Later, much later, Mama, her hair and clothing redolent with the fragrance of maple sugar, brought Nell's supper.

"How sweet," Mama said, bending down to the nursing kittens. "How tender."

Until her father took them off to drown them. But she was not going to let that happen. "Papa cannot come in here anymore."

"But why, Nellie? Papa loves you, as I do, and he wants to see you."

Nell pulled herself into a sitting position. She was not going to discuss the kittens' fate. That would only provide a reminder to fuel her father's intentions. "Papa can see me downstairs. I'll come to the parlor in the evenings."

When Nell said she'd stir from her room, Mama's face brightened as if she believed Nell might be turning a corner. "To the parlor? How wonderful. Maybe we'll make a fire and start a jigsaw puzzle. Oh, and Nellie, when we were washing up today, we found the *ring*."

"What ring?"

"Anson's—in a bar of our kitchen soap."

"The ring? Well, it's his, so give it back to him. I have no use for it."

"Oh, Nell," Mama wailed, looking downcast again. "Why can't you struggle?"

Nell sipped broth from a mug. "I will never marry Anson Tanner."

Tears welled up in her mother's eyes. "We know that, Nell. That's been decided, for once and for all."

"No spring wedding? No summer wedding in the orchard? Or in fall, when the trees are in color?"

"No, no—not for you. Not if you don't wish it. But you must bestir yourself, try to regain your health."

"Why?"

"Because you have so much to live for."

Nell laughed bitterly. The laugh made her hands shake, and broth slopped over the edge of the mug. She put it down, but she didn't wipe the broth off her quilt. "Do I?"

Tears had begun to course down Mama's cheeks. "Yes, for yourself and for us. Even if you, just now, don't love yourself, *we* love you."

Nell reached out. Soon she and Mama were holding one another. They were both crying. "But it's too hard, Mama— what you have to do. The same things over and over. You said once you didn't want me to lead your life, and I don't want to. I can't bear it. How can you?"

Mama pushed Nell away and held her at arm's length. "I said that, and for you I meant it. But, Nell, the question Papa told you to ask, the one you asked the night of 'the turn' about me. About how *I* feel. This is my life, and I *chose* it. I chose it over Boston, over a life with more ease and fewer hardships."

"But why?"

"Because, dear one, I care for your father and for the farm. The sugaring, putting up food, making candles or soap, stuffing a down pillow, weaving a basket, the change of seasons . . ."

Nell didn't answer.

"Besides," Mama continued, "the only thing I detest here, truly detest, is the laundry!"

"And being poor."

"Being poor? We're not poor, Nellie. Short of money—yes. Particularly in a bad growing season. Being poor, however, is a different thing. It's hard here, but it's that way for everyone. City, country, rich, or poor."

Nell frowned. "You said you didn't want me to live your life, and that's why I was to marry Anson Tanner."

"Well, I didn't. And I don't, honeypot. Too many of the things I love here are things that you resent. But to marry Anson—I see now and we all see—was not the right solution."

"And what is?"

Mama's eyes filled with tears again. "I wish I knew," she murmured. "But, even more, I wish you knew, because then you might put up some semblance of a struggle."

Mama left then. Nell sat staring vacantly around her candlelit room. She was so weak she couldn't imagine going to college or off to Boston. Why had she thought those were things she wanted to do? How could she help others when she wasn't able to help herself?

Downstairs, she heard the sounds of supper being prepared. She smelled warm maple syrup and knew her family was celebrating the sugar season by having stacks of pancakes at night instead of in the morning. Her mouth watered, but she stayed where she was.

She could hear them talking, too, their voices punctuated by Eliza's laughter.

"But that's what Anson wants."

"Not until Nell gets better."

"That will be too long."

"Liza!"

"Does Nell care? Does she? She dropped his ring into the soap!"

"Hush! No more. Dr. Sternhagen said we must wait."

Nell shut out their voices and began to look about her small upstairs room—the bed, the quilt, the chair, the chifforobe, the rag rug, the tie-back window curtains, her frocks hanging in the closet. Beneath them, the tabby and her kittens slept peacefully.

Nell sighed and let herself sink deeper into her pillows. She had promised to go downstairs to see Papa. But it would take a good deal more strength than she possessed. What was it Dr. Sternhagen had said? That they'd have to wait? Well, Nell was waiting. And, at this moment, that seemed to be about the only thing she could do.

Saturday, February 24, 1900

As Nell waits, the world around her moves on. The days are growing longer. The fields and woods she sees from her window have begun to trade their drab browns for hazel tones tinged with green. And the tabby's kits have opened their eyes, started to explore the confines of her room. Although Papa hasn't come for them yet, Nell knows he will. That's why she keeps a nightly vigil. Some midnight, he will steal them and end their lives in a bucket of water.

When Mama brings food for Nell, she also brings a dish of table scraps for the tabby. But the tabby is dissatisfied. Sometimes she shakes off the nursing kits and prowls about the room. She seems hungry. So this morning, when Papa, Mama, and Eliza were outside, Nell made her way down to the kitchen.

Once there, she leaned against the counter and examined the contents of the ice chest. She rejected the leftover ham. Too salty. Behind it she found a chicken carcass Mama was saving for soup. The tabby liked chicken.

Nell picked at the carcass, tearing off slivers of dried-up meat, putting them on a plate. In the chest cavity, she found the heart and the gizzard. Pleased, she added them to the pile. Next, she came upon the shriveled, overcooked liver. As she was about to lay it on the plate, an impulse took hold of her and she began to nibble at it. She was angry with herself for succumbing to this compulsion, yet she kept taking bites of the liver, chewing, swallowing as if it were the tastiest thing she'd ever eaten.

"I thought you didn't eat dark foods," a voice said.

Nell, alarmed to be caught at such a degrading activity, started to shake. It was Papa who had spoken to her. Nell dropped the meat. She didn't know what to say. If she told Papa she was gathering provisions for the tabby, he'd probably march upstairs and snatch the kits.

Papa spoke again. "You wouldn't be shivering, Nell, if you'd remembered a wrap or slippers. It's foolish to endanger yourself further—"

"Stop," Nell was cold, but she didn't want to discuss this any more than she wanted to talk about the chicken liver. "Don't."

"As you wish," Papa said, with an air of resignation. "I shan't disturb you. I only came in because the cow has a sore shank and I needed a clean rag for the salve."

The liver taste in Nell's mouth was disgusting. She could feel bits of the rubbery brown stuff stuck between her teeth. Besides, standing up was making her dizzy. She wanted to flee to her room but wasn't sure she could do so without blacking out. Then Papa would have to carry her. Then he'd take the kittens.

She pushed her lank hair behind her ears. "I'm sorry."

"For what?"

"For everything."

"Then do something about it," Papa said, bending down and reaching for the rag bag.

"I can't."

Papa raised one eyebrow. "Perhaps not."

Nell was leaning against the counter. Only its firm wooden top was keeping her upright. "Do you hate me?"

"No."

"What is it, then?"

"The way you are. I can't bear to see you like this."

Nell wrinkled her forehead. "That's what Rob said."

Papa stuffed a white rag into his pocket and returned the rest to their sack. "They heard from him, you know."

"Who?"

"The Hoffmans. From Rob. He's in California. He asked about you."

Rob's name stirred only bitterness inside her. "He wanted to know if I'd died yet. If I was dead."

"Stop, Nell. Please stop. I can't endure this."

"Nor can I."

Later, as the kits tumbled on top of her quilt, raking it with their needle-like claws, she knelt at the window and looked out. Papa, his shoulders sagging, was repairing a hinge on the side gate. Mama and Eliza were at the fire pit, stirring the contents of a large cauldron.

"I hate not knowing when," Eliza complained.

"You must have patience."

"But, Mama, it could be months or years."

"We must wait."

"No, I won't! And if Anson . . ."

Nell stopped listening, but she watched them hypnotically. They were dyeing shirts and nightclothes. The dingy garments went into the vat a grayish yellow and came out an intense, flawless blue. From Nell's vantage point, it looked as if her mother and sister were stealing fragments of the sky to pin on the clotheslines.

Midafternoon, Anson Tanner, his mother, and Jewel came to pay a call. Nell had been asleep when they arrived. But she awakened when she heard voices in the parlor below her. She didn't move. She stayed where she was, staring at the black diamond in the center of her quilt. There was something she needed to do. What was it?

After a while, she went to the window and peered out again. Ludie, beginning to look perceptibly thicker about the middle, was down near the woods, feeding the birds. Tobias and Mr. Hoffman were preparing a field for early planting. In the orchard, Nell saw Eliza. Jewel was with her. Jewel was as wizened as ever, but Eliza—laughing, chatting, smiling—was round and lovely.

"Look at her. The worse I get, the healthier and more robust she becomes."

As Eliza pushed at the swing, something sparkled, caught a fragment of light, and flashed it back toward Nell. Nell pressed closer to the glass, hoping to discover what it had been, but the phenomenon didn't repeat itself. Only later, after nightfall, did it become clear.

Eliza was going to marry Anson Tanner. That's what Mama said when she came in with Nell's supper. What Nell had seen was the glint of his ring on her finger.

"When?" Nell asked.

Mama gestured vaguely. "We don't know. She doesn't graduate until June. It's not yet settled."

They were waiting to see what happened to her. It would, of course, be unseemly for Eliza to wed when Nell was so ill. How inconsiderate she was being. Eliza, never a patient person, was having her future dictated by her sister's fate. Nell didn't know whether to laugh or cry, but she found she was too numb to do either.

"Eliza must hate me."

"Nellie! That's a terrible thing to say."

Nell had said and done so many terrible things in the last year that one more hardly mattered. Now Nell knew why her sister sewed and sang about the house. If Nell had paid attention, at least half the whispers she'd listened to might have supplied her with clues. It was perfect— almost too perfect. Her sister would get to be Mrs. Anson Tanner. But not as long as Nell was spreading a pall over their lives.

In case Nell thought she was being too harsh in her judgment of her sister, she had it reconfirmed that evening as she leaned against the door of her room while Mama and Eliza were in the upstairs hall saying good night.

"It would be nice in the summer," Eliza said, "but early, before it gets too warm."

"Sssh, Liza. You must be patient."

"Well, I'm not. I'm impatient. Nell's inhuman. She's inconsiderate, cruel to you, to Papa, to all of us. She's taken leave of her senses."

"She's sick," Mama said.

"Well, I'm sick of her. Mr. Holmes, in *Elsie Venner*, says a hysterical girl is a vampire who sucks at the blood of the healthy people around her."

"Liza! I won't stand for that kind of talk."

"But, Mama, Nell's illness is infecting us all."

"Stop! Don't!"

"Why don't you face the truth? Because you don't wish to see how poorly she's doing. Look at her—a puff of wind could blow her over. She isn't even strong enough to sew on her quilt anymore."

Mama sighed.

"That beautiful quilt," Eliza murmured. "What's going to happen to it?"

About the fate of the quilt, Nell felt indifferent. She was ready to let go, she could let go, but not quite yet. There was something unfinished. Whatever it was pulled at her. But what was it? What?

As she stumbled toward her bed, one of the kits pounced from behind and sunk its teeth into her ankle.

"Oooo . . . ouch."

Hopping forward, Nell eased herself into a chair. Then she bent her foot sideways to examine it. There were twin slits, each beaded with a drop of bright blood. She was amazed to find she felt pain. She was also surprised to discover that her body remembered how to bleed.

Saturday, March 3, 1900

Before sunup, as Nell was keeping watch over the tabby and her kittens, an eerie, grating sound began to penetrate her consciousness. The sound was coming from somewhere beyond the house. For a while, she listened to the repetitive scrape-scrape. Then, finally, piqued by a wave of curiosity, she rose from her bed. A glance out the window provided no clue. It was too dark to see. Nor could she pinpoint the exact location of the disturbance.

"Maybe they're fashioning my coffin."

It wasn't the sound of the saw which she heard, but she assumed that other tools were also necessary to make a coffin. At last, unable to endure the noise a moment longer, she donned her boots, a coat, and Rob's cap. Then, moving as soundlessly as possible, she went downstairs and stepped outside.

From the yard, she still couldn't identify the scraping sound or its source. It seemed to come from behind the barn, but she wasn't sure. Moving with care, aware of spasms of pain in her spindly limbs, Nell headed in that direction.

As soon as her eyes accustomed themselves to the half-light, she could make out the farm buildings and the dusting of snow that had fallen a few days before. When she rounded the corner of the barn, she was distressed to find nothing there. The noise persisted, though, somewhere past where she stood.

Taking small steps to conserve energy, Nell pressed on. Up the road, behind the Hoffmans' barn, she discovered Ludie, seated on a stack of raw lumber, surrounded by an ax and half a dozen knives. In her hands she held a metal file, and between her knees a short-handled hatchet.

As Nell watched, Ludie—apparently oblivious to everything—stroked the hatchet over and over and over with the side of the file. Her intensity was fearful, and Nell wanted to leave. But she was tired. Besides, the sight of the girl rasping away with such determination pierced her apathy.

At last, Nell spoke. "What are you doing?"

Nell expected Ludie to start with surprise. She thought the girl might stand up and threaten her with the hatchet, or stalk off. She was wrong.

"What does it look like?" the girl replied, not bothering to raise her eyes.

Nell, too weary to stand any longer, let herself sink down on the lumber beyond the ax and the assortment of knives. "That's not what I meant. I meant what—or *why* are you out here before sunup, sharpening tools?"

"Better than staying in there," the girl replied, jerking her head in the direction of the cabin she shared with Tobias.

Nell nodded. To ward off the morning chill, she pulled the cap down over her ears. Ludie stopped filing long enough to test the sharpness of the hatchet with the tip of a finger and the edge of a fingernail. Apparently satisfied, she put it down, reoiled the file, and reached for one of the knives. Angling it precisely, Ludie scraped it back and forth against the file. After a while, she abandoned the file and began to hone the knife against a sharpening stone.

Edgy from the irritating screech of iron against stone, Nell forced herself to say something. "Are you happy about the baby?"

"There ain't going to be one," Ludie replied.

"No baby? But Mama said . . . and Mrs. Hoffman said . . ."

"Well, they're wrong. I lost it. A few days back."

"Lost it?"

"In the privy."

Nell shuddered. "The privy?"

"Yes."

"What happened?"

Ludie shrugged. "One early morning, when my belly cramped, Toby told me to quit thrashing around. So I went out."

"Alone?"

"Yes," Ludie said. "But it was just a blob, a bloody fishy thing. I was glad to see it go."

Again Nell shuddered, imagining the awfulness of sitting in a dark privy and having a baby—a tiny, half-formed one—expelled from one's body onto the dank matter below. "You didn't have anyone to be with you?"

"Who?"

Who, indeed? Nell felt a surge of pity. "That's very sad."

Ludie glanced up from her work. "Is it? Well, suit yourself. I ain't sorry. Ain't told no one, either."

"Why?"

"Why should I? It's my body, even if he don't always know it."

Nell rubbed her hands together to keep them from tingling with cold. "But he's your husband. You married him."

"Had to," Ludie replied. "I was three months along and showing, so my people threw me out." She reversed the angle of the knife she was holding. "But he's an animal, and I'd watch out for him if I was you."

Nell turned toward Ludie. "No—not now. He's stopped looking at me."

"That's what you think," Ludie said bitterly. "He looks. And he'll mount anything that moves, long as it's halfway female. Me, the spaniel, a chicken, the mare. My dressmaker's dummy if he could figure out a way. And, yes, even a skeleton like you!"

Nell's heart was beating in a strange, irregular way, as if it had been cut loose from its mooring and was thumping on its own somewhere inside her bony chest. "But if you dislike him so, why don't you leave?"

"And go where?" the girl asked.

Shaking now, Nell crossed her arms across her chest and hugged herself. "D-do you ever just think you'd be better off dead? That's what I tell myself, what I think."

"No!" Ludie answered without hesitation. "Not me. I don't want to die. I want to ride in a motorcar. See the ocean. And other things. Right now, I've got no choice, so I stay here. But maybe one day"—she paused to give the knife a particularly vicious thwack against the stone—"maybe one day I'll kill him."

"You'd kill?"

"Why not? Either you do unto others, or they do unto you."

"But you don't need to *kill* Tobias. You could run away. Go work in a mill."

"In a mill? So I could stand on my feet all day? Die like that, instead of like this?"

Nell leaned forward. "Listen, Ludie, I can help you. I know I can. Find you a place to stay, a job. I can, truly. Just give me a chance."

Ludie turned and examined Nell. "You?" She hooted derisively. "Look at you, you scarecrow. You can't help no one."

Nell, too cold and too agitated to sit any longer, rose unsteadily to her feet. "But . . ."

Whatever it was she meant to say, the words never came. She glanced around. While she and Ludie had been talking, it had grown light. Now the eastern sky had a peachy-pink glow. Billows of bluish mist hung in the lowlands. It looked as if they were on an island, one of many in a vast, roiling sea.

Nell wanted to show Ludie the facsimile of the ocean. She wanted to tell the girl how achingly beautiful the morning was. But, somehow, she didn't think Ludie would understand or agree. It was hopeless, quite hopeless. She had nothing to offer.

Nell turned and began to walk back toward her house. She'd only taken a few steps when Ludie called out after her. "Wait!"

Nell paused. She looked back. "What?"

"That quilt thing you were making, the bright, pretty one you showed me, that's got places for you and your people on it?"

"What about it?"

"Is the center still black and ugly?"

Nell nodded. "Yes."

"What are you fixing to put there?"

"Nothing."

Ludie put down the knife and the stone. "Well, listen,

if you ever change your mind, you might put me there—smack dab in the middle of that quilt. Because I'd like, just once, to be someplace as beautiful as that."

Perhaps Nell had been wrong. Perhaps Ludie would have understood that the fog looked like an ocean, that the morning was breathtaking to behold. She might have marveled, too, that the sun's first rays were slanting across the fog and above it, turning the bits of snow and frost into caches of radiant gems.

But Ludie had mentioned the crazy quilt. And that put an end to the possibility of having any further conversation with her. Nell lowered her head. She didn't want to see Ludie or the way in which the colors of the morning had begun to simulate the brilliant tones of her quilt.

A voice was pounding in Nell's head when she reached her room again. "Dare you, dare you, dare you."

"No. I won't. I can't. It's over."

But, even as she spoke, Nell found herself shooing the tabby and her kits off the top of the crazy quilt. She dropped to her knees and began to rummage through the black ash basket. When Nell had thought that the quilt, like her life, was over, she'd been wrong.

She wasn't finished yet. Almost, but not quite. She still had more to do. At first, she pawed through the basket, trying to unravel the nest of tangled threads. Then, forcing herself to slow down and be patient, she extracted every single hank of red thread. Because that was what she wanted—all the varied, flaming, rusted, shining, bloody colors of red.

Saturday, March 3, 1900

The black diamond in the center of Nell's quilt isn't empty any longer. Using a thick, nubby plush stitch, she has filled it with a red flower—both vivid and dark—that she calls an amaranth. She's not sure she's ever seen any amaranths, but she's read about them, and she imagines they look like the flower she has created. The amaranth is especially important because of its other name: love-lies-bleeding.

"Done." Nell clipped the last thread. "That's for Ludie."

Then, examining the amaranth, she decided that there was too much intimidating black around it, so she took other, brighter threads and embroidered them across the velvet until she'd fenced the flower in with fancywork, fashioning a square within a square.

As she was admiring her work, Eliza brought in her breakfast tray. "Oh, Nellie," she said. "I do like your quilt."

"I know," Nell replied.

Shuffling her feet, Eliza twisted a taffy-colored curl around one finger. Nell felt as if her sister was about to pounce on her and wrest the quilt from her hands. But Eliza showed restraint, and without speaking again, she hurried from the room.

After Nell sampled her breakfast, she dumped the rest into the bowl under her bed where the tabby and her kits could enjoy it. Food was of no concern to her, because there was something important she needed to do. Put her name on the quilt.

Using a length of scarlet thread left over from Ludie's amaranth, Nell took hold of the empty rectangle of mauve taffeta at the bottom of her own block. There, working with a triple thread, she outlined four letters.

N - E - L - L. Nell.

Looking at it, she smiled grimly. Now that the quilt said NELL, it was—this horrible, heavy thing she'd come to despise—finished. She could put it to rest forever.

"Nell." Aware for the first time that her name had a somber homonym, she pronounced that, too. "Knell. A knell for Nell. That's what they'll ring when I'm gone. Nell's knell."

What she longed to do was lie down under the completed crazy quilt and never move again. But she was strangely exhilarated. Thoughts were reverberating in her head, pulling at her, nagging her. Even though the quilt was finished, she was not.

She washed, dressed, and brushed through her ragged, unclean locks. Then, stuffing the quilt into its basket, she walked from her room. She was at the top of the stairs when she heard Eliza's voice.

"But Mama, she could give it to us—to Anson and me—for a wedding gift. Then, if she gets stronger, she can make another quilt!"

Mama didn't answer, but Nell did. As she made her way down the steps, she gave her sister a scathing look. "I shall never make another quilt."

Then, moving past Mama and Eliza, she went into the utility room. There, she picked out a cauldron, seven bottles with dark cork stoppers, and some other supplies. Soon, she stood at the yard fire pit, feeding a fire, waiting for the water in the cauldron to come to a boil.

Mama and Eliza didn't venture outside. But Nell, without turning her head, sensed that they were watching her from the kitchen windows. They wanted to find out what she was about to do. Was Papa there also? Or was he watching from the doorway of the barn?

The sun was out, the low mists had burned away, and a sharp wind was blowing from the north; yet close to the fire it was warm. Nell waited and waited. At last, the cauldron began to boil. Taking the bottles she'd brought from the utility room, she began to uncork them and pour their contents into the cauldron.

"Red. Green. Yellow. Blue. Orange. Brown. And black. These will make a very black black."

Nell was adding dye to the cauldron, all the bottles of homemade and store-bought dye that Mama kept in the utility room. The water turned a dark, smutty tone. Unmoving and unmoved, Nell stood waiting for it to come to a second boil.

When it did, Nell—forcing herself to remember that she was looking at fabric scraps *bought* at Jordan Marsh—extracted the quilt from its basket and, with great care, lowered it into the cauldron. It was so bulky that black liquid slopped over the top and made the fire sputter and hiss.

Nell added more wood. She took a long stick and began to stir, so that the dye would absorb into every fiber of the silk and velvet patches, into each polychrome strand of thread. For what seemed like a long time, she remained where she was, feeding the fire and rotating the cauldron's contents.

Finally, as satisfied as she was ever going to be, she used

the stick to lift the quilt from the cauldron. She let it slide from the stick to the ground, where it lay black and steaming.

When Nell thought it was cool enough, she took hold of the weighty, swollen thing and began to wring the excess dye from it. As she twisted, it drenched her skirt and apron, staining them black. But Nell didn't care. She didn't need that blue skirt or that apron. Her hands stung. She'd scalded them, because the heavy fabrics, made heavier by water, had retained astonishing pockets of heat.

After a while, too exhausted to keep extracting water from the quilt, she dragged it over to the clotheslines. With one last surge of energy, she pinned it up. Then, panting, she stood back to survey her work.

The crazy quilt on which she'd spent nearly a year of her life was dark now. Yet, the longer she stood there looking at it, the more surprised she was. The quilt should have been uniform in color—a solid, coal black. It was, instead, a quirky mélange of blacks, bronzes, buffs, mahogany browns, and other charred, sooty tones. Here and there the evidence of a plaid or a stripe presented itself. Different fabrics had absorbed the dye in different ways.

For a moment, hesitating, she tried to decide if she wanted to return the quilt to the cauldron again. She blew on her stinging hands. She shook her head.

"No, it's fine. That was the best, the very best I could do."

For hours that day, Nell lay in her room, watching the kittens, waiting for the quilt to flap itself dry. She tried to keep her mind vacant of all thoughts, but odds and ends, bits of useless miscellany, kept tumbling about in her head.

Even the child's rhyme about birthdays and days of the week.

At noon, Mama, pale as if she'd seen a ghost, came in with a bowl of potato soup. She seemed to be on the verge of tears.

By way of contrast, Nell felt calm and dry-eyed. "Mama?"

"What, honeypot?"

"Was I born on a Wednesday?"

Mama shook her head. "No, Thursday," she said, beginning to edge toward the door. "It was a Thursday, because the doctor was at his lodge meeting, and Papa had to go fetch him."

Mama left. Nell was alone again—except for the tabby and her kittens. They'd become rambunctious, their temperaments too frivolous to match Nell's. They scrambled up the curtains, burrowed under the covers, played hide-and-seek in the laundry basket. They were too big to drown, but they were also too tame to fend for themselves in the wild.

"Who is going to find homes for you?" Nell pressed her smarting palms together.

As she was admonishing the kittens, Mrs. Tanner and Jewel, driven by their stableman, arrived to pay a call. Soon, Nell heard them below in the parlor. After a while, she heard Eliza and Jewel out in the yard. Nell leaned against the window frame to watch them.

Jewel was being whiny and difficult. "Please, please . . . it's one of the bestest things here."

Eliza snapped at Jewel. "Not 'bestest.' Say 'best.' Besides, the henhouse is a filthy place. You're wearing a nice frock, and you should keep it clean."

Two months ago, Eliza had stood up for Jewel's right to be a child. But now, as an engaged woman, her sister was beginning to treat Anson Tanner's daughter exactly as his mother did.

"Poor Jewel." Then Nell noticed someone else in her line of vision. "Poor Ludie."

Ludie was hauling a basket of ironing from her cabin toward the Hoffman house. Tobias, carrying nothing but an empty burlap sack, was a step or two ahead. It was terrible, so terrible. Maybe she hadn't been born on a Wednesday. Maybe none of them had, but everywhere Nell looked, she saw woe.

The afternoon dragged on endlessly. At last, the Tanners left. By then, the sun was low on the horizon, which was banked with dark clouds. There would be no glorious sunset. The sun would sink like a dull orange stone and disappear from view.

When Nell could procrastinate no more, she made her way downstairs and out into the yard. The quilt was soggy and damp in places. But Nell couldn't wait any longer. She unpinned it, draped it around her shoulders, and headed inside.

She didn't want to see anyone. But Papa materialized in front of her with a pail of steamy milk.

"Now that you've managed to destroy the quilt," he suggested, "perhaps you'll find something else to do. You've never been a quitter. Are you going to start now?"

Nell didn't answer. Instead, she plodded into the house, up the stairs, and into her room. She removed her dye-stained clothing and changed into a clean white night-dress.

Next, she extinguished her candle. Out the window, she

could see the sliver of a new moon poised above the cloud bank on the western horizon. Unwilling to look at it, she lowered her eyes and shooed the kittens off the bed. Then she sat down and took hold of the variegated black crazy quilt.

With great care, she arranged it—patting out every last pucker and wrinkle—over her feet, along her legs, over her thin, thin body. At last, leaning back, she pulled it up close to her chin and slid her arms beneath the quilt. She clasped her scalded, tingling hands on top of her chest.

Then, taking a deep breath, Nell lay there and waited. She heard an owl hoot. The Hoffmans' spaniel was barking. But that was not all she heard. No matter how she tried to blot them out, voices called to her.

"I dare you, dare you, dare you!"

"One day I will kill him as he is killing me."

"Granny Tanner says I make her head ache."

Other voices, too. Grandmother Shaw laughing to think Nell had assembled patches from a Jordan Marsh kit, urging Nell to remember there were more important things to do.

Papa repeating: "Everything you do to yourself, you do to us, too."

Ludie declaring she wished to see the ocean.

Jewel amazed that maple syrup comes from a tree.

Anson Tanner saying Nell had "a strong spirit and a joy" about her which she should not lose.

The new minister quoting Mr. Emerson's belief that "the only gift is a portion of thyself."

Eliza angling for the quilt. Mama, suffering, dying herself as she watched Nell dying.

"No! Stop talking. All of you. Stop! I shall not listen.

This is the end. The end of Nell. Nell's knell. Nell is going to die now."

No voice dared to contradict her. There was no sound, except one.

"Meow."

Then again, closer and more plaintive, "Meow . . ."

Tears began to stream from Nell's eyes. Who would look after the kittens? After Jewel? After Ludie? After Mama? After the many others that Grandmother Shaw struggled to help? This wasn't right. She didn't have to give *all* of herself, only a portion. Nell—no, not Nell—it wasn't Nell lying under that quilt waiting for death to come.

It wasn't *her*. It was *ME*. I was the one—I, Eleanor Sara Edmonds, was trapped there, unable to move, unable to change anything. Death was going to stalk in at *my* door and take *me*, for I'm Wednesday's child, and I'm "full of woe." But wait, I'm not Wednesday's child. Dr. Sternhagen was at his lodge meeting. I'm *Thursday's* child, and "Thursday's child has far to go."

Well, death is some kind of long, long voyage. Death is far to go. But so is life. Something inside me was welling up, surging, exploding.

I sat up and took hold of the dark, heavy quilt.

"No, no, no . . ."